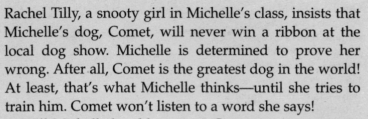

Rachel Tilly, a snooty girl in Michelle's class, insists that Michelle's dog, Comet, will never win a ribbon at the local dog show. Michelle is determined to prove her wrong. After all, Comet is the greatest dog in the world! At least, that's what Michelle thinks—until she tries to train him. Comet won't listen to a word she says!

Will Michelle be able to turn Comet into a superstar dog by show time? Or will Rachel have the last laugh?

STEPHANIE

Stephanie's excited about the dog show, too. She's helping get Comet ready by taking him for long runs in the park. Stephanie loves going to the park—and not just for Comet. At the park, Stephanie met a cute boy named C.J., who asked Stephanie on a date.

Stephanie couldn't be more excited. Until she finds out that C.J. has a big secret—one that could turn her best friend against her. Should she spill the beans and risk losing a date? Or hide C.J.'s secret and risk losing a friendship?

FULL HOUSE™: SISTERS books

Available from MINSTREL Books

FULL HOUSE™

Sisters

A Dog's Life

DIANA G. GALLAGHER

A Parachute Press Book

Published by POCKET BOOKS
New York   London   Toronto   Sydney   Singapore

A MINSTREL PAPERBACK *Original*

A Minstrel Book published by
POCKET BOOKS, a division of Simon & Schuster, Inc.
1230 Avenue of the Americas, New York, NY 10020

A PARACHUTE PRESS BOOK

Copyright © and ™ 2001 by Warner Bros.

ISBN: 0-671-04093-6

First Minstrel Books printing April 2001

10 9 8 7 6 5 4 3 2 1

A MINSTREL BOOK and colophon are registered trademarks of Simon & Schuster, Inc.

Printed in the U.S.A.

A Dog's Life

MICHELLE

Chapter
1

Awesome! Michelle Tanner stopped short in front of the bulletin board outside the Fraser Elementary School cafeteria.

Cassie Wilkins, one of Michelle's best friends, walked into her. "Oof! What is it, Michelle?"

Mandy Metz, Michelle's other best friend in Mrs. Yoshida's fourth-grade class, leaned toward the poster Michelle was staring at. She read it out loud. " 'Children's Dog Show at the Canine Center in Burnsville. Obedience, agility, and fun events for kids of all ages and dogs of all kinds.' "

"It's two weeks from tomorrow." Michelle's eyes shone. She thought of her golden retriever,

Comet. *Comet will love being in a dog show,* Michelle thought.

"Wait a minute." Cassie's eyes narrowed. "You're not going to enter Comet, are you?"

"Sure." Michelle beamed. "Comet and I watch that dog-training show *Unleash the Hounds!* every day. I've already taught Comet some of the basic obedience stuff. If I train him every day, he'll be great! I bet he'll even win a blue ribbon."

Mandy hesitated. "But Comet doesn't *always* do what you tell him."

"Unless you feed him biscuits," Cassie added.

"Comet can do it. I know he can," Michelle insisted.

"Yeah, if he *wants* to. Comet definitely has a mind of his own." Mandy giggled.

Michelle had to agree. Comet did do what he wanted to do most of the time. Still, the dog was better behaved now that she had taught him to come, sit, and stay. *Even if he doesn't obey* all *the time,* she thought.

"We just don't want you to be disappointed, Michelle," Cassie said. "I mean, what if Comet totally refuses to listen in front of all those people?"

2

"Yeah," Mandy agreed. "Maybe putting Comet in a dog show isn't such a good idea."

"I already entered him," Michelle said, and winced. She hadn't thought about Comet messing up in front of an audience! "There was a sign-up form in the paper this morning. I filled it out and put it in the mailbox."

"Oh." Mandy shrugged. "Then I guess it's too late to talk you out of it, huh?"

Michelle nodded. Comet was a great dog and she wanted everyone to know it. "I can work with Comet every day after school. And all day on weekends. Tomorrow's Saturday—I can start then."

"So you're really serious about this?" Mandy asked.

"Yep." Michelle nodded again. "I know Comet can do it!"

"Well, since you've made up your mind . . ." Cassie grinned. "Can Mandy and I help?"

"That would be awesome." Michelle brightened. It was great to know that she could always count on Cassie and Mandy no matter what.

Mandy looked at the poster again. "They have a couple of categories that Comet could win: most handsome dog, the dog the judges would most like to take home, and best biscuit catcher."

"Comet is a sure winner in *that* one!" Cassie laughed.

Michelle nodded. Comet loved it when she scratched him behind the ears and took him for walks, but the thing he loved *most* was when she fed him dog biscuits.

Mandy kept reading. "Obedience isn't Comet's strong point, but what's agility?"

"I don't know." Michelle shrugged.

"No way! Don't tell me!" a voice called out. Michelle turned as Rachel Tilly walked up beside her. Rachel glanced at the dog show poster and raised an eyebrow.

"Don't tell you what, Rachel?" Michelle asked. Rachel was in Mrs. Yoshida's class, too. Rachel always said exactly what she thought and usually gave Michelle a hard time.

"You're *not* thinking of entering your dog in the Children's Dog Show, are you, Michelle?" Rachel asked.

"Yes, I am," Michelle said. "It sounds like fun."

Rachel rolled her eyes. "But your dog doesn't

have a pedigree. And you don't even know what an agility class is."

Michelle frowned. That was true, but what was Rachel's point?

"My dog, Bonnie Blue, is a registered sheltie and she's had *professional* obedience training," Rachel explained.

"So? Comet is really smart," Michelle countered. "And *I've* been training him for months."

"If I were you, I wouldn't bother," Rachel said. "Comet will be out of his league. He can't win a ribbon against *real* show dogs."

Michelle tensed. *I can't let Rachel insult Comet and get away with it*, she thought.

"Don't count on that, Rachel." Michelle forced a smile. She was not going to let Rachel get to her. "Comet is a lot smarter than you know. He'll win at least one ribbon. Maybe more!"

"Right." Mandy's eyes flashed. "Comet is a very handsome dog."

"And the best biscuit catcher in San Francisco," Cassie added.

Rachel laughed. "Just don't blame me when you make a fool of yourself, Michelle. I tried to warn you."

All three girls frowned as Rachel walked into the cafeteria.

"What are you going to do, Michelle?" Mandy looked worried. "Now Comet *has* to win a ribbon."

"Yeah." Cassie sighed. "If he doesn't, Rachel will never let you forget it."

Michelle set her jaw. Her friends were right. *If Comet doesn't win a ribbon, I'll look like a total loser! And Rachel will tell everyone.*

"Comet *will* win," Michelle vowed. "I'm going to make sure he does."

Chapter
2

After school Michelle dragged three flattened cardboard boxes down the back steps and across the Tanners' backyard.

"Hey!" Joey called out from the kitchen door. "Aren't those the boxes your dad was saving to ship Christmas presents in this year?"

Michelle glanced back over her shoulder.

Joey was her father's best friend. After Michelle's mother had died, Joey and her uncle Jesse moved in to help her dad take care of Michelle and her two older sisters, D.J. and Stephanie. Now Uncle Jesse's wife and their twin boys, Alex and Nicky, lived in an apartment in the

7

attic of the big house, too. Aunt Becky was a co-host on the TV show *Wake Up, San Francisco* with Michelle's dad, Danny Tanner.

"Uh, yeah, but I need them." Michelle gave Joey her best pleading look. "It's really important. Dad won't mind."

"You're probably right." Joey smiled. "Anything I can do to help?"

Michelle dropped the boxes and ran back to the steps. She picked up *Good Dog*, the dog-training book she had taken out of the school library that afternoon.

"I'm making an agility course." Michelle showed Joey the picture in the book.

Joey looked puzzled. "Why?"

"So I can train Comet for the Children's Dog Show," Michelle explained. She pointed to the white, upside-down cones in the book. "Do you have anything I can use instead of these cone things? Comet just has to walk around them."

"Let's see." Joey tapped his chin for a moment, then snapped his fingers. "How about wastepaper baskets?"

"Perfect! Will you get them for me?" Michelle

started past him back into the house. "I have to go get the twins' desk chairs to use in the agility course."

"What?" Joey put an arm across the open door to block Michelle. "Did you ask Alex and Nicky?"

"I can't—they're at the park with Uncle Jesse." Michelle stared at the ground a moment, then looked up. "But they won't mind because I'll promise to play games with them for a *week* after the dog show."

"Wait!" Joey moved his arm when Michelle tried to duck under it. "What if they *do* mind?"

Michelle groaned. "Then I'll give the chairs right back."

Joey nodded. "Okay."

Michelle darted through the doorway when Joey moved aside. She raced up to the attic apartment. Stephanie and D.J. weren't home yet, but she hoped they would do some of her chores so she could spend all her free time training Comet.

They'll help me, Michelle thought as she carried the first small chair down to the yard.

Because I'll be sure to make it up to them after the dog show.

After Michelle got the second chair outside, she helped Joey empty the wastepaper baskets into a trash bag. When she had everything outside, she checked the dog-training book. The chapter on agility had instructions on how far apart and how high all the obstacles should be. She used the picture as a guide to put everything in the right place.

I'll start with the easy part first, Michelle decided. She placed the two chairs about four feet apart with the backs facing each other. Then she placed a broom across the chair tops. The jump was about eighteen inches high, just like the one in the book.

Next she put the wastepaper baskets upside down in a line. She didn't have a tape measure so she had to guess that they were about eight feet apart. Comet would have to learn to weave in and out of them.

Michelle glanced at the dog. He was sleeping by the back steps. *Good,* she thought. *He'll be rested and ready to go when I'm done.*

The ramp was harder to build. Michelle

looked at the picture in the book and sighed. It was a white bridge with ramps on both ends.

"I'll just have to do the best I can with what I've got." Michelle placed one end of her hard plastic sled on top of a cinder block Uncle Jesse had left in the backyard. *Comet will just have to pretend there's a ramp on the other side,* Michelle thought.

Michelle had saved the really hard part until last. She dragged the flattened boxes to the far side of the yard and unfolded them. She left both ends of all the boxes open.

Comet woke up and stretched. He walked over and cocked his head, watching as Michelle pushed the end of the first box into the end of the second, larger box.

"Don't worry, boy. The agility class is really easy once you know what to do." Michelle patted Comet.

The golden retriever flopped down on his stomach and rested his chin on his paws.

Michelle then stuffed the end of the second box into the end of the third box. The three connected boxes formed a kind of tunnel. She moved the tunnel to the left side of the yard. It wasn't as pretty as the one in the book, which was white with blue and red stripes, but it did the trick.

If Comet learns to go through my tunnel, Michelle thought, *he'll be able to crawl through anything.*

Michelle glanced at the dog. "Okay, Comet! Ready?"

Comet raised his head and thumped his tail.

At least he looks interested. Michelle grinned. Obedience training had been kind of boring. She was sure, though, that teaching Comet to go through the agility course would be a lot more fun.

"Come on, boy! Let's get started!" Michelle clapped her hands.

Then she remembered that the trainer on *Release the Hounds!* used the same command every time she wanted a dog to get ready to work. *Maybe I should use the right obedience commands all the time with Comet,* Michelle thought. *That way he'll get agility and obedience training at the same time!*

Just to be sure she got it right, Michelle flipped through the book to the chapter on obedience. She quickly read the page that listed the basic commands. The book used the same commands and hand signals she had learned from the dog trainer on TV.

Michelle put the book down and stood up. "Come, Comet!" She waved Comet over with her hand.

Comet slowly stood up and stretched, then walked over with his tail wagging. Encouraged, Michelle clipped a leash to his collar. According to the book, she had to lead him through the course a few times so he would know what she wanted him to do.

"Stay," Michelle commanded, holding her hand out, palm down, at Comet's nose.

Comet yawned and sat down.

"No! You're supposed to stay standing up, Comet." Michelle pulled on the leash to get the dog back on his feet. "Now pay attention. You're going to love this."

Comet trotted beside Michelle to the right side of the yard. When she stopped, Comet started to lie down again. "No, no, no!" Michelle pulled him back to his feet. "Just follow me, Comet," she said. She shortened the leash and consulted the book. "Heel!" Michelle patted her leg, then she began walking the course.

Michelle wove her way around the waste-paper baskets, but Comet walked right past them in a straight line.

"Hmmm. Let's try that again." Michelle backed up, then started walking again. When she went around the first basket, Comet started to follow. Then he suddenly jumped to the other side of the basket.

Michelle pulled on the leash with one hand and patted her leg. "Follow me, Comet. Come on. Heel. That's a good dog." Suddenly Michelle froze. She had forgotten that she usually patted her leg when she wanted Comet to play!

Uh-oh, Michelle thought.

Comet jumped toward Michelle. She almost fell over backward when he put his front paws on her chest and started licking her face.

"No, Comet!" Michelle tried to sound stern, but that was hard to do when she was giggling. Then she had a bright idea. *Comet thinks I'm playing! So I'll just turn the agility lesson into a game.*

A Dog's Life

Michelle kept patting her leg as she scurried around the wastebaskets. Comet followed her around the first three and knocked over the fourth. When she stopped, Comet kept standing.

"Sit!" Michelle pointed to the ground, using the signal she had seen in her book and on TV. Then she pushed on his hindquarters with one hand while continuing to point with the other. Comet sat. She patted his head. "Good dog!" she cheered. "Three out of four isn't perfect, but it wasn't bad for your first time."

Comet scratched his ear with his hind leg.

"Okay. Let's do the jump next. Heel!" After tugging, Michelle got Comet moving again. She jogged toward the broom she had stretched between two chairs and leaped over it. When Comet saw the broom, he stopped dead, yanking Michelle's arm and making her halt abruptly.

"Come on, boy. It's not that high!" Michelle tugged on the leash and patted her leg again.

Comet dropped to the ground and tried to crawl under the broom. Michelle put her hand on his nose to stop him. "No, Comet. Like this."

Michelle led Comet back a couple of steps. When she leaped over the broom again, Comet ran around the *outside* of the chair. Michelle decided to keep going.

She ran for the cardboard-box tunnel and fell on her knees to crawl through. Comet dug in his heels and pulled back.

"It's okay, Comet." Michelle was careful not to lose patience with her dog. She managed to turn around inside the tunnel so she was backing out the other end. She crawled backward and pulled on the leash. "Come on, boy! You can do it."

Comet lunged in the opposite direction. The leash flew out of Michelle's hand. Sighing, she backed out the rest of the way and stood up. Comet stared at her from the other end of the cardboard boxes.

"Come on, Comet. I know you can do this." Michelle squatted down and looked through the tunnel. "Come on, boy! Come, Comet!" She waved her hand.

The golden retriever ducked his head to look inside the box tunnel. He gave a little whine. Then he leaped into the air and landed on top of the boxes. The cardboard tunnel collapsed.

"Oh, no!" Michelle threw up her hands. "Look what you did."

Comet sat on the flattened boxes, wagging his tail and panting. He looked pleased with himself.

"Well, the boxes aren't broken," Michelle said with a sigh. "I guess I can fix this later. Let's try the ramp." Grabbing the dog's leash, Michelle ran for the ramp. Comet bounded along beside her. When Michelle stopped at the end of the sled that was on the ground, the dog kept running. He almost pulled her off her feet.

"Oops! Wait a minute, Comet!" Michelle let go of the leash before she fell. As soon as the leash was dropped, Comet turned and came bounding back down the ramp.

He isn't being bad on purpose, Michelle realized. *He just doesn't know what I want him to do.*

"Okay, Comet." Michelle picked up the end of the leash and made Comet sit. Then she gestured at the sled and explained. "You walk up the ramp and down the other side. Only we don't have a ramp on the other side, so I guess you have to jump."

Comet cocked his head and gave a little "woof."

Michelle was just about to answer, when she heard the back door opening.

"What's going on here?" her dad asked as he walked outside. He frowned when he saw all the stuff Michelle had strewn around his neat and tidy backyard. Danny loved it when everything was in its place and hated when things were messy.

"It's my practice agility course, Dad," Michelle explained. She walked over to him, dragging Comet behind her. "For the Children's Dog Show at the Canine Center in Burnsville. I'm going to enter Comet."

Danny blinked in surprise. "You're going to put *our* Comet in a dog show?"

Comet flopped down on the ground and stretched out on his side.

Michelle unclipped the leash from his collar and nodded. "I've got two weeks to train him."

"Well, a little training certainly won't hurt," Danny said.

"That's what I thought." Michelle grinned. "Comet can enter the beginner obedience and agility classes. And some of the events are just for fun, like the catching-treats contest. Plus they give ribbons in every single event. Comet's sure to win one."

"Well, I think it's a great idea," Danny said, encouraging her. "Whether Comet wins a ribbon or not." He picked up Michelle's book from the ground and looked at the cover. *"Good Dog: Basic Training for Your Best Friend."*

"I found it in the school library," Michelle said.

Danny studied the picture of the real agility course, then glanced at the practice course Michelle had built. "You did a good job, Michelle, considering that you had to use what you could find around the house."

"Thanks, Dad." Michelle sighed. "It's sort of the same as a real course, but not exactly."

"Maybe I could help you build one that's more like this." Danny pointed to the picture. "If you want help."

"Want it?" Michelle beamed. "I'd *love* it!"

"Great!" Danny smiled. "We'll go pick up

what we need in the morning. By tomorrow afternoon, you'll be all set."

Michelle threw her arms around her father's waist. "You're the best, Dad. And so is Comet. I just know he's going to win a blue ribbon. You wait and see!"

STEPHANIE

Chapter
3

"Tell me you're kidding!" Stephanie Tanner held the phone between her chin and her shoulder. She was trying to finish the Saturday morning breakfast dishes and talk to Allie Taylor and Darcy Powell at the same time.

Three-way conference calling is so cool! Stephanie thought as her two best friends filled her in on the latest middle-school gossip.

"I am totally not kidding," Darcy said. "Susan Jefferson broke up with Tommy Franklin last night."

"What happened?" Stephanie was astounded. Tommy and Susan had been going out for weeks.

She grabbed the phone to keep it from falling as she stuffed the last plate in the dishwasher.

"Apparently, Tommy was a total jerk at the movies," Allie explained. "He was throwing popcorn at his friends and the manager kicked him and Susan out."

"How embarrassing!" Stephanie poured detergent into the washer cups and closed the door. She turned on the machine and sat down at the table.

"Yeah," Darcy said. "That's why Susan told him to get lost the minute they walked out of the theater."

"Thank goodness Chris isn't like that," Allie said.

Stephanie smiled. Allie had totally flipped over her new boyfriend. Stephanie and Darcy hadn't met him yet because Chris went to a different school.

"So when do we get a chance to hang out with this great guy, Allie? This afternoon?" Stephanie asked.

"I can't," Darcy said. "I've got a family picnic I've got to go to."

"That's okay, Darcy," Allie said. "I have a lot

of chores to do today so I can go out with Chris tonight."

"Where are you going?" Stephanie asked.

"Chris has tickets to some outdoor jazz festival," Allie replied. "Not that I like jazz that much, but I promised I'd go with him."

Stephanie was disappointed, but she didn't let on. "I bet you'll have a great time."

"Only because I'll be with Chris. Even if the jazz is boring, he's so gorgeous that I can just look at him." Allie giggled. "What are you going to do this weekend, Steph?"

"I'm not sure," Stephanie said. Her homework was finished and she had the whole day free. *With nothing to do because Allie and Darcy both have plans!*

"The only thing going on here is that Dad and Michelle are building some kind of dog-training course," Stephanie reported. She had volunteered to do the dishes so Michelle could go shopping with their father for supplies.

"For Comet?" Darcy sounded skeptical.

"Well, he's the only dog we have." Stephanie laughed. "Michelle entered him in the Children's Dog Show at the Canine Center in

Burnsville. All she could talk about yesterday at dinner was winning a blue ribbon."

"But Comet hardly ever does what you tell him," Darcy said. "I don't mean that in a bad way. It's just that—"

"I know what you mean, Darcy," Stephanie interrupted. "Winning with Comet is probably hopeless. Michelle is going to be so disappointed when she doesn't win any—oh!" Stephanie jumped when something cold touched her leg under the table. She rolled her eyes when Comet pushed his wet nose into her hand, asking her to pet him.

"Are you okay, Steph?" Darcy asked.

"Fine." Stephanie grinned. "Comet's nose is cold."

"Hey, I've got to go," Allie said. "My mom is calling me."

"Me, too." Darcy sighed. "I have to help my mom get the picnic stuff together. Catch ya later."

Stephanie exhaled as she hung up the phone. *So what am I going to do for the rest of the day?*

Comet nudged Stephanie's hand when she stopped scratching behind his ears.

"I could watch cartoons with the twins,"

Stephanie told the dog. "But to be honest—cartoons aren't my thing anymore."

Comet barked. Then he trotted to the door in the living room and glanced back at her.

"What?" Stephanie watched the dog, puzzled.

Comet barked again and wagged his tail.

"Do you want to go for a walk?" Comet turned in a circle and barked again.

"I guess that means yes," Stephanie said, getting to her feet. *Why not? I don't have anything better to do, and Michelle won't need Comet until she and Dad finish building that training course.*

Stephanie yelled out to Michelle that she was taking Comet for a walk. Then she got the dog leash from the junk drawer.

Comet took one look at the leash and bolted happily for the front door.

Stephanie led Comet across the park to the new Canine Play and Run area on the far side of the baseball field. Stephanie had heard about the area where dogs could run off the leash, but this was the first time she had brought Comet.

"Whoa! Pretty cool, huh, boy?" Stephanie

glanced down. Comet was more interested in sniffing the fence around the baseball field than in the park, but she was really impressed.

A chain-link fence enclosed the huge canine playground. The large green meadow was dotted with big shade trees. The water fountains had built-in ground-level basins for dogs. Several park benches and picnic tables were scattered under the trees.

Stephanie's arm ached because Comet had tugged and pulled so hard on the long walk to the park. *I should have remembered to put treats in my pocket like Michelle does*, Stephanie mused as she sat down on a bench. *Then maybe I could get him to heel.*

Comet spotted several other dogs romping with one another or playing fetch with their owners. He whined and pulled at the leash.

"All right. Let's play." Stephanie picked up a stick and unclipped Comet's leash. Comet loved to chase sticks.

Comet ran in circles, barking and jumping up and down, trying to snatch the stick from Stephanie's hand.

"Down, boy!" Stephanie giggled, then heaved

the stick as far as she could. Comet ran after the stick, picked it up, and started to run back.

"Come on, boy!" Stephanie bent over and clapped her hands. "Bring it to me!"

Comet charged toward Stephanie, then veered just as she reached out to grab the stick.

"Comet!" Stephanie lunged toward the dog, but Comet bounded just out of reach with the stick clamped in his mouth. Every time she straightened as if she were giving up, Comet came closer, but every time she tried to snatch the stick, the dog scrambled away again.

"Dodger dog," Stephanie observed, "but I want that stick." On her fifth try, she managed to grab the end of the stick, and Comet let go.

Comet started barking and jumping so Stephanie would throw it again. She threw the stick and smiled as Comet bounded across the freshly mowed grass to fetch it.

While she waited, Stephanie glanced around. All the other dogs in the park seemed so well behaved compared to Comet. An elderly couple sat on a bench with a beagle napping at their feet. A boy wearing a college T-shirt was playing Frisbee with a shaggy white-and-black Border collie that caught the red disk in midair and returned it to his owner every single time. A young woman jogged with her yellow Lab at her side. A small group of slightly older-looking kids sat at one of the picnic tables. Three dogs romped around them.

Another boy, who looked to be about Stephanie's age, was tossing a ball for a big black poodle. The poodle brought the ball back to him, sat, and dropped it in his hand.

The boy looked right at Stephanie and smiled.

Even from a distance, Stephanie could tell the dark-haired boy was cute. She smiled at him, then realized Comet was bounding back toward her. She reached out to grab the stick, expecting him to jump aside.

Instead, Comet dropped the stick and leaped toward her.

Caught off balance, Stephanie stumbled and fell on her back in the grass. Comet started licking her face.

He just wants to show me how happy he is to be at the park, Stephanie thought. *But still, this is so embarrassing!* She squirmed out from under the dog. She didn't dare look at the boy with the black poodle.

A Dog's Life

As soon as Stephanie was on her feet, Comet playfully pranced away again. She shook her head and laughed. "I hope you're happy now that you've made a complete fool of yourself—and me!" she called after the dog.

"That's a great-looking golden retriever," a boy's voice said.

Stephanie whirled around to see the boy and his black poodle standing a few feet away. "Uh—thanks," she replied.

He's even cuter up close! And nice, too, Stephanie thought. The black poodle was sitting perfectly still on the boy's left side. "The Canine Play and Run is great, isn't it?" he said. "I bring Jasper almost every day." The boy pushed a shock of dark brown hair off his forehead. His blue eyes were as bright as his friendly smile. The poodle continued to sit quietly beside him. "What's your dog's name?"

"Comet." Stephanie took a step closer to the boy. "You have a gorgeous dog, too."

Comet stuck his nose into a small hole in the ground, then started digging.

Stephanie pulled him away by the collar, reattached his leash, and whispered, "Comet, no!"

She didn't think the park people would appreciate dogs digging up the grass even if they were in the canine section.

"Thanks. Jasper's pretty cool." The boy grinned with pride.

"He's really well trained," Stephanie said. Jasper still hadn't moved.

The boy looked at Jasper. Then he raised both his arms into the air. "Okay!" he said to the poodle.

Jasper jumped to his feet and started sniffing the ground, acting, well, more doglike than he had a moment ago.

"What was that all about?" Stephanie asked.

"*Okay* means he can do what he wants," the boy said, "until I call him back."

"I'm impressed." Stephanie smiled.

Suddenly Comet yanked his leash out of her grasp and ran across the lawn toward the dogs playing by the picnic table.

Stephanie gasped. "Comet! Come back, boy!"

Comet ignored her. A yellow Lab broke free from its companions and came up to sniff noses with the golden retriever. Within seconds, they were playing together.

"Looks like Comet made a friend." The boy glanced past Stephanie toward the black poodle, who was following his nose toward the baseball field. "Jasper, come!"

Stephanie watched in amazement as Jasper instantly wheeled around and ran to the boy.

"How did you teach Jasper to obey like that?" Stephanie asked with genuine interest. "Comet never does what I tell him."

"It just takes patience and repetition. You have to work with your dog every day." The boy hesitated. "I could give you some pointers if you want. Just basic obedience stuff."

"Would you?" Stephanie grinned. *This is great! If I can train Comet, Michelle will have a better chance of winning a ribbon at the dog show!* she thought. Plus, instead of ruining her chances to get to know the boy better, Comet's bad behavior had actually helped Stephanie.

"I'd love that," she told the boy. "I'm Stephanie Tanner."

"My friends call me C.J."

"I'll be grateful for any advice I can get." Stephanie glanced at Comet. He and his new dog friend were sitting in front of the picnic table. The older-looking kids were tossing them bits of their lunch.

Besides, Stephanie thought, *if Comet and I spend enough time with C.J., I might just get myself a new boyfriend!*

"Why don't you go get Comet, and then we can get to work," C.J. suggested.

"Thanks," Stephanie said. She watched as C.J. walked Jasper over to the big oak tree and ordered him to lie down and stay. Jasper did exactly as he was told. She ran over to grab Comet's leash. She had to drag him away from the yellow Lab.

"Okay. Ready to start?" C.J. asked when she got back.

"The sooner the better," Stephanie said. "Comet has a lot to learn!"

MICHELLE

Chapter
4

"What do you think, Michelle?" Danny asked.
He dropped his hammer in the toolbox and
stepped back.

Michelle looked at the ramp her father had
just finished building. They had bought three
pieces of plywood at the lumber store and two
wooden step stools with only two steps on them.
Danny had used all that to construct the ramp.
He had set the step stools four feet apart and fastened one of the pieces of plywood on top of
them—sort of like a bridge. Then he nailed the
other two pieces of wood in place. They rested
on the steps to form a ramp on each side.

"It's great, Dad!" Michelle beamed. "It looks just like the one in my book—except it isn't white."

"Does it have to be white?" Danny asked.

"Nope. In fact, I like it plain." Michelle jumped up to unpack the canvas play tunnel they had bought at the toy store. It was just the right size for Comet to run through. *And when I'm done training Comet, the twins can play with it*, Michelle thought happily.

"Do you want this where the cardboard-box tunnel was?" Danny asked. He carefully cut the protective plastic wrap off the collapsible tunnel.

Michelle nodded. "That's where the book said it should go."

Michelle ran up and down the ramp to test it. *After Dad's helped me so much, Comet just has to win a blue ribbon in the dog show,* she thought.

"Wow!" Michelle watched as her father stretched out the blue canvas play tunnel. It was three feet high and ten feet long with wire hoops inside to keep it round. "If Comet jumps on this one, it won't squish. It will just bounce back to the way it was."

"A definite plus." Danny walked over to the wastepaper baskets Michelle had gathered. He pulled his tape measure out of his back pocket. "These are supposed to be eight feet apart, right?"

"Yep." Michelle watched as Danny measured the distance between the wastepaper baskets. He had put brown paper grocery bags around the house for the family to use instead of the baskets.

After Danny finished measuring, he stood up and looked around with a satisfied smile. "Well, all we have to do is finish the jumps and you'll have a brand-new and improved agility course!"

"Yay!" Michelle jiggled with excitement. "I can't *wait* to try it out with Comet." *Whenever Stephanie brings him home*, she thought. Her sister had been gone all afternoon with the dog.

Michelle carried the twins' chairs over to the steps while Danny brought out the cinder blocks he'd gotten at the store. He was going to use those and some white plastic pipe to make two jumps so that Nicky and Alex could have their chairs back.

"I just hope Comet thinks this is as much fun as you do, Michelle," Danny said.

"He will. Comet is really smart. He can learn all this agility stuff," Michelle assured him. "Plus, I'm going to keep training him in obedience. And tricks! And catching treats."

"That's an awful lot to teach him in just two weeks," Danny observed.

"Yeah," Michelle agreed, "but I really want to win a blue ribbon at the dog show."

"That would be nice." Danny slipped a plastic pipe through the holes in the cinder blocks. "But remember the Tanner motto: Winning isn't as important as having a good time and doing your best."

"I know," Michelle said. She'd heard the Tanner motto a million times before. She knew her father was trying to make sure she didn't get her hopes up. Michelle couldn't help it, though. *I know Comet and I can do it*, she thought with determination.

"I want you to be proud of us, Dad," Michelle told him.

"I'm already proud of you." Danny smiled and closed his toolbox. "But if you need any help training Comet, just ask, okay?"

"Thanks," Michelle said. "But the book says

that only *one* person should train a dog so the dog doesn't get all mixed up."

Danny nodded. "Well, we certainly don't want Comet getting more confused than he already is."

"Nope." Michelle glanced around the yard. The new practice obstacles her dad had made were perfect. "Thanks for helping me with the agility course, though, Dad. It's super!"

"It looks almost professional, doesn't it?" Danny folded his arms and nodded with satisfaction. "You're all set to start training Comet tomorrow."

"Tomorrow?" Michelle stared at him. "But I want him to try it today!"

"I know, but Stephanie isn't back yet," Danny said. "And after such a long walk, Comet will need a good night's rest."

No way, Michelle thought. *With Stephanie hogging all of Comet's time, I'll never get him trained for the dog show!*

Chapter
5

Stephanie smiled at C.J. They had been working for an hour and a half. He had spent the first hour showing her all sorts of commands and tricks with his poodle, Jasper. Now it was Comet's turn.

"We'll start with some basic obedience commands, okay?"

"I'm ready."

"For starters, hold Comet on a short leash and say 'sit,' " C.J. explained. "As you say the word, make a downward slashing movement with your hand. If he doesn't do it, use the hand signal again and push on his rump until he does."

"That sounds easy enough." Stephanie slid her hand down the leash to shorten it and ordered Comet to sit.

Comet cocked his head sideways, unsure what Stephanie was trying to say. Stephanie pushed on the backside of the dog, and Comet sat.

"Wow!" C.J. looked impressed. "That was great."

Stephanie gave him a sheepish grin. "He's kind of used to that one. We make him sit to get treats at home."

"Then you're already ahead of the game." C.J. looked impressed. "Except you shouldn't reward him with treats until *after* you're through working."

"Oh." Stephanie nodded. "But then why should Comet cooperate? I mean, if he doesn't get anything out of it."

"Pet him and tell him he's a good dog." C.J. glanced back at Jasper. "Jasper loves that."

"Okay," Stephanie said. "What next?"

"Tug on his leash and say 'heel.' Point down at the ground by your foot, and then start walking," C.J. told her. "Walk in a big circle and make sure you keep him right by your side. Don't let him pull ahead."

Not so easy, Stephanie thought as she tightened her grip on the leash. Comet liked to rush ahead. *He's always in a hurry no matter where he's going.*

"Okay, Comet—"

"Don't say 'okay'!" C.J. shook his head and waved his arms. "That's the command to let him know he can do what he wants."

"Oh, right." Stephanie wilted. "But how am I going to do this without saying *okay?*" she asked. "I always say *okay!*"

"Just say 'Comet, heel!' " C.J. suggested.

"Got it." Taking another deep breath, Stephanie tightened her hold on the leash again. "Comet, heel!" She pointed to her foot and took a step forward.

Comet didn't budge. He just adjusted his rump on the ground.

"Heel, Comet!" Stephanie pointed again and pulled on the leash.

Comet whimpered.

Stephanie felt kind of guilty. *This can't be much fun for Comet*, she thought. *But if I don't do this, then Michelle won't have* any *chance of winning a ribbon.*

"Come on, boy. Heel." She tugged on Comet's leash with all her might, pulling the dog to his feet.

"Great!" C.J. nodded his approval. "You have to let your dog know who's boss."

"Right." Stephanie agreed halfheartedly. Under C.J.'s direction, Stephanie made Comet sit, then heel again—over and over. After fifteen minutes, Stephanie had to admit to herself that Comet wasn't the only one who seemed bored, but she didn't want to give C.J. the wrong impression. He really seemed to take this dog-training stuff seriously.

Finally Comet had had enough. He yanked his leash away from Stephanie and bounded over to the yellow Lab by the picnic table. The other dog took off across the grass. Comet ran after it with his leash trailing behind him.

"Uh . . . 'okay!' " Stephanie commanded a few seconds too late. "I guess we're done here for today." She frowned at C.J.

"Don't be upset, Stephanie," C.J. said. "He did fine for his first lesson."

Except this isn't his first lesson, Stephanie thought.

"Listen, I've got to go anyway. I have something to do today, and I'm already late." C.J. signaled Jasper to join him. The black poodle trotted up to his side and sat down. "Will you be here Monday—after school?" C.J. asked.

"Absolutely." Stephanie grinned. "Thanks for not giving up on Comet."

"Well, I can't do that. Then I wouldn't have a reason to hang out with you again." Giving Jasper the "okay" signal, C.J. waved and ran toward the baseball field. "Bye, Stephanie!"

Thrilled, Stephanie hurried off in the opposite direction—toward her own dog. *C.J. wants to see me again*, she thought. *He likes me. This is awesome!*

The young woman who owned the yellow Lab was sitting on a bench at the picnic table. The Lab and Comet were lying at her feet, panting after their long run.

"Hi." Stephanie smiled as she stooped to pick up the end of Comet's leash. "I hope Comet isn't bothering you too much."

"He's no problem at all." The young woman

smiled and patted Comet's head. "Comet and Morrin seem to be becoming good friends."

"Is that your dog's name?" Stephanie leaned over to let the Lab sniff her hand. "Hi, Morrin." She looked up at the woman. "I'm Stephanie."

"Nice to meet you, Stephanie," the woman replied.

"Cathy!" a young man called. Stephanie turned and saw someone waving from the parking lot.

"Oops! Gotta go!" Cathy stood up. "See you soon, Comet and Stephanie." She headed toward the young man, Morrin trotting by her side.

Comet whined.

"Sorry, boy," Stephanie told her dog. She made sure she had a tight hold on the leash. "Morrin has to go home, and so do we."

"Heel," Stephanie said as she started toward the park exit. Comet walked calmly right by her side. He even sat down without being reminded when she stopped before crossing the streets.

Wow! Looks as if I made some progress today after all! Stephanie thought. *With Comet and C.J.!*

Maybe Michelle's chances for a ribbon at the

dog show weren't hopeless after all. Now that Stephanie had C.J. to help her train Comet, she couldn't wait for Michelle to try him on the new agility course. She bounded up the steps of her house, happy that she'd been able to help.

Michelle threw open the front door. Stephanie stopped in surprise. Her little sister looked totally furious.

"Where have you been with my dog?" Michelle demanded.

Chapter
6

Michelle crossed her arms and glared at Stephanie. Stephanie had been gone for half the afternoon. *Saturday is almost over and I haven't trained Comet at all,* she thought.

Comet pulled at his leash to get in the door.

"I took him to the park." Stephanie unclipped the leash and Comet bolted inside. "You know, Comet isn't only *your* dog, Michelle," Stephanie added. "He's the family dog, and I'm part of the family."

"But I've got a few hours less than two weeks left until the dog show!" Michelle threw up her arms. "I can't train him if he's not here."

"Well, he's home now." Rolling her eyes, Stephanie edged past Michelle and went inside, too. "I was just trying to help, you know."

Michelle tried to calm down. Stephanie hadn't deliberately taken the dog to keep Michelle from training him. So being mad at her wasn't fair.

Maybe Stephanie doesn't know how important the dog show is to me, Michelle reasoned.

She took a deep breath. "I'm sorry I got mad," she said. "But if I don't teach Comet how to do all this stuff, Rachel and her dog are going to beat Comet and me at *everything!*"

"Rachel's entering the dog show, too?" Stephanie asked with a frown. "Is she giving you a hard time about it?"

"Not really, but Rachel thinks she's going to win because Bonnie Blue was trained by a *real* dog trainer." Michelle followed Stephanie into the kitchen.

Comet had drunk all the water in his bowl. Now he was lying on his stomach, eating the dog kibble left over from breakfast.

Stephanie put the leash on the counter, opened the refrigerator, and got herself a soda. "Well, when you think about it, what difference does it make?" she asked. "You're in the dog show to have fun, right?"

"Well, that's how I felt when I sent in the entry form." Michelle squatted down to pet Comet. "But then I told Rachel that Comet was *sure* to win a ribbon, and you know Rachel. If Comet doesn't win something, she'll make sure everyone in school hears about it for the rest of the year."

"You can't worry about Rachel, Michelle." Stephanie pulled on the tab, popped the soda top, and grinned. "Besides, I have a feeling that Comet is going to do a wonderful job at the show."

"Great." Michelle stood up and reached for the leash. "So Comet's all mine until the dog show, right?"

"Whoa! Who said that?" Stephanie asked.

"I have to train him *every* day," Michelle explained.

"I didn't agree to that, Michelle," Stephanie protested. "I want to take Comet to the park every day."

"You can't!" Michelle gasped. "Comet will

never learn how to run the agility course if he doesn't practice. And he's not exactly perfect on obedience, either."

"But there's this great—" Stephanie broke off. "I mean, maybe I can help. If I can take him to the park . . ."

"You *can't* help, Stephanie."

Michelle didn't want to argue, but Stephanie obviously didn't know anything about training dogs. Michelle was about to explain that according to her training book, only *one* person was supposed to train a dog, when—

"Do you want Comet to lose, Michelle?" Stephanie's eyes flashed. "If that's the case, then fine!"

"No, but—" Michelle sagged when Stephanie stormed out of the kitchen.

The next morning, after getting dressed, Michelle looked for Stephanie. She wanted to apologize for their fight the day before. Her sister didn't know about the one-trainer rule, but she was right about one thing. *Comet is the family dog,* Michelle thought. And *Good Dog,* the training book, had said that dogs couldn't work *all* the time. They needed time off to have fun just like people.

"Stephanie!" Michelle ran into the living room. Her sister was sitting on the couch, flipping through TV channels with the remote.

"Steph, I've got an idea," Michelle said.

Stephanie hit the Mute button. "What is it?"

"Well, I decided you're right about Comet being the family dog." Michelle didn't pause to take a breath. "So what if you take him to the park on Mondays, Wednesdays, and Fridays and I have him the other four days?"

Stephanie didn't respond for a second. Then she nodded. "Okay. That works for me."

"Cool! I've got to start training Comet right now because tomorrow is Monday. See you!" Michelle raced back into the kitchen and grabbed the leash.

"Come on, Comet. We've got a lot of work to do." Michelle had to tug hard to get the dog to stand up. "I know you don't like to work, boy, but you'll be glad when you win a blue ribbon."

Comet followed Michelle out the door and sat down when she stopped at the bottom of the steps.

"Good boy!" Michelle was thrilled. That was exactly what he was supposed to do. *Maybe he does remember the obedience training we did last time.* She hoped so. Then they could spend more time on the fun stuff like tricks and agility.

"Let's try the whole routine," Michelle said. "Just like they do it on TV."

Comet started to lie down.

"Not yet, Comet." Michelle pulled him back up. "I'll tell you when to lie down."

Michelle had paid really close attention to the dog trainer on *Unleash the Hounds!* so she knew just what to do. She stood still with the dog on her left side and shortened the leash. Then she gently tugged on Comet's collar to get his attention.

"Heel, Comet!" Michelle patted her leg with her hand. She started walking.

Comet hesitated, then walked by her side, tugging a little on his leash.

Not bad, Michelle thought. *But here comes the hard part.* She approached the edge of the yard. She concentrated on placing her feet just right to change direction. She tried to picture the maneuver in her mind.

Turn my right foot out, Michelle reminded herself. *Bring my left foot around and start off again with my right foot.*

Michelle grinned when she found herself walking back toward the house with Comet still heeling by her side. *Wow! It worked!*

As Michelle circled the yard, Comet started to lag behind.

"What's wrong, boy?" Michelle asked. She held her hands, palms up, in front of Comet.

Comet immediately sat down.

"Wait! Not yet," Michelle yelped. Comet started to lie down.

Michelle quickly decided to take advantage of the moment. She put her right hand in front of the dog's nose and moved it toward the ground. "Down, Comet!"

Comet jumped up and let out a bark.

Michelle frowned. Did Comet have his signals mixed up or something? Maybe she should try another command. She put her right hand level with the dog's face, palm side down. "Stay, Comet! Stay!"

Comet remained perfectly still.

"Good dog. Stay!" Michelle dropped the leash

and backed up a few steps. She held her right hand out. "Stay."

After a minute Michelle walked back around the dog, and then stopped so he was on her left side again. *That's the first time he did that right!*

Overjoyed, Michelle decided to try something else. Comet had never gotten this command right, either. She put her hand out again and said, "Wait."

Crossing her fingers, Michelle backed up and waited for another minute. "Come, Comet! Come!" She waved her hand, slashing it through the air.

Comet rolled over on his side and closed his eyes.

Michelle just stared at him. *Comet's not confused. He's probably just tired after playing in the park all day,* she thought with dismay.

Michelle gazed at the wonderful agility course her father had built. Comet wouldn't even get up and walk. There was no way Michelle was going to get him to jump and climb the ramp or crawl through the tunnel.

"You must be tired," Michelle told her dog.

"So maybe we can try it later when Dad can watch. After you take a nap."

Now that she had made a deal with Stephanie, Michelle didn't want to waste any of the time she had with Comet. She got the dog brush out of the junk drawer and spent forty-five minutes brushing him.

Comet dozed through most of the grooming.

Michelle said, "Roll over" when she pushed him over to brush his other side. She hoped he'd remember the command for the competition. When she was done brushing him, his golden coat gleamed.

I'll have to brush him every day for the most handsome dog competition, Michelle thought as she walked back toward the house. She was absolutely certain that Comet had a good chance to win that, too.

Just as she reached the door, Michelle heard Comet give a little bark. She spun around. "Oh, no!"

Comet was rolling in the compost heap of dirt and leaves that Aunt Becky kept in the corner of the yard. When he stood up and shook himself, his beautiful, shiny coat was covered in leaves,

twigs, and mud. He certainly didn't shine anymore.

Michelle sank down on the steps. *Maybe
twelve more days isn't long enough to get Comet
ready for the dog show. Maybe I need twelve more
years!*

Chapter
7

On Wednesday Stephanie left school with Allie and Darcy. She was eager to get home because it was her day to take Comet to the park.

"Why don't you guys come with me?" Stephanie asked her friends.

She hadn't told them about C.J. because he hadn't shown up at the park on Monday. She didn't want to make a big deal out of the new boy in her life until she was sure he liked her.

"I can't today," Darcy said. "My mom has the flu, so I have to go home to help out."

"I'm sorry your mom is sick, Darce," Stephanie said. "I hope she feels better soon."

"Yeah, me, too." Darcy smiled. "It seems like the three of us haven't done anything together for a month."

"I guess I have been spending a lot of time with Chris lately." Allie shrugged.

"We don't mind," Stephanie said. She didn't want Allie to feel guilty about seeing her new boyfriend so often. "You should go out with Chris as much as you can, Allie."

"Right." Darcy nodded. "I mean, Chris obviously likes you as much as you like him, doesn't he?"

"Absolutely!" Allie's eyes sparkled. "He told me last Saturday that I'm the *only* girl he wants to hang out with."

"Really? That is so cool." Stephanie felt glad that Allie had found such a great guy.

"Are you seeing him today?" Darcy asked.

Allie shook her head. "No. My mom's taking me shopping for some new clothes." She gave Stephanie a sheepish grin. "So I can't go to the park, either. Sorry, Steph."

"That's okay." Stephanie smiled. "If I had a choice between getting new clothes and hanging out with a dog, I'd pick clothes, too."

After Allie and Darcy left, Stephanie hurried home to get Comet. This time she didn't mind that Comet pulled on the leash on the way to the park. Stephanie was even more eager to get there than he was.

I know C.J. has a perfectly good explanation about why he didn't show up on Monday, she thought. *Not that he owes me an explanation*, she reminded herself. *I don't have an exclusive thing going with C.J. like Allie has with Chris.*

A squirrel sitting on the lawn darted away when Stephanie and Comet passed.

Comet barked and sprang, yanking his leash out of Stephanie's hand.

"Comet!" Frustrated, Stephanie chased the dog to the bushes where the squirrel had taken refuge. Comet ran back and forth in front of the bushes, sniffing at them and whining because he couldn't find the squirrel. Stephanie picked up the leash and hauled the dog back to the sidewalk.

I should be grateful he didn't run away, Stephanie thought. *Comet never used to be so out of control.* She chewed on her lip, remembering how uncooperative the dog had been during

Michelle's training session the day before. *He's getting worse instead of better. And Michelle still doesn't want any help.*

Stephanie understood that her sister wanted to train Comet herself—that way she could feel proud of her accomplishment at the dog show. *But Michelle's training isn't working. If this keeps up, she won't have any chance of winning a blue ribbon. C.J. is her only hope of getting Comet ready in time*, Stephanie thought.

Still, she didn't want to make Michelle feel bad.

I know! I just won't tell Michelle that C.J. helped train Comet. And then she can enjoy her victory.

A dog barked out the window of a passing car.

Comet pulled on the leash and barked back until the car turned the next corner.

If there is *a victory*, Stephanie thought with a sigh. She decided to cheer herself up by thinking of C.J.—she couldn't wait to see him.

Stephanie jogged past the baseball field with her fingers crossed, but she quickly realized that C.J. and Jasper weren't in the Canine Play and Run area. In fact, there were only two dogs there, and they belonged to a couple of high school kids.

Stephanie stayed calm and positive. C.J. didn't go to John Muir Middle School. Maybe his school dismissal time was later than hers.

Morrin isn't here, either, Stephanie noticed. It was a good opportunity to get in some quality practice time if Comet wasn't distracted.

Stephanie was sure she remembered everything C.J. had shown her on Saturday. Taking up the leash, she began walking, holding Comet on a short leash so he would heel. Then she stopped walking.

"Sit, Comet," Stephanie said as she came to a halt.

Comet kept going until he reached the end of the leash.

Stephanie remembered what C.J. had told her to do. She pulled Comet back and held her hand, palm down, over his head, the way C.J. had shown her.

Comet started to sit, then changed his mind. He looked at her and whined.

"What's the matter?" Stephanie was frustrated but tried not to let it show. *Jasper sits auto-*

matically whenever C.J. calls him to his side, she thought. *But Comet's acting like he doesn't have a clue what to do.*

Stephanie frowned. When Michelle was working with the retriever in the backyard yesterday, Stephanie hadn't noticed her using a hand signal to make him sit. She had just tugged on the leash and told him to sit.

That's it! Stephanie realized. *Michelle isn't doing it right.*

She looked down at Comet. "Well, boy, we have our work cut out for us," she told him. "I have to get C.J. to train you the right way without letting Michelle catch on. Her dog-show ribbon depends on it."

In response, Comet buried his nose in his paws.

"Sulking won't help, Comet." Stephanie gave him a stern look. The dog seemed so sad, but she had to be firm. "No playtime until we're done working."

Just as Stephanie was about to try again, she saw C.J. and Jasper running across the meadow.

"Sorry I'm late, Stephanie!" C.J. stopped and doubled over to catch his breath.

"Well, I'm just glad you're here!" Stephanie didn't ask where he had been on Monday. *It's not like we're going out or anything*, she thought.

Jasper bounded toward Stephanie, wagging his tail. He was happy to see her.

"So how's it going?" C.J. asked.

Stephanie sighed. "He's the most stubborn dog on the face of the earth. I've been working with him, but he doesn't seem to understand what he's supposed to do."

"Don't get discouraged." C.J. smiled. "The key is repetition. You just have to keep doing everything over and over."

"Well, I'm ready whenever you are," Stephanie said brightly.

"No time like right now."

C.J. called Jasper to his side. Stephanie watched closely as C.J. held his palm out, face-down, and moved it slowly toward the ground. "Down, Jasper," he ordered. Jasper immediately lay down. Next, C.J. pointed at Jasper and ordered him to stay while he walked away. C.J. walked all the way to the baseball field, but Jasper didn't move until he came back and gave him the "okay" sign.

Stephanie groaned. "Comet hasn't even figured out that he's supposed to sit every time I stop. I'm not sure he's ready for 'down' and 'stay.'"

"Maybe not, but I just wanted to show you what to do," C.J. explained. "So you know when Comet is ready."

"Okay." Stephanie tried to sound cheerful, but she wasn't sure she'd remember everything. *And if I have a hard time, how can I expect Comet to figure it out in just ten more days?*

Then Stephanie spotted Cathy and Morrin coming into the park from the jogging trail on the other side of the meadow. Comet noticed his new friends, too, and took off at a run toward them.

With a sinking heart Stephanie watched him run away. "He's hopeless."

"Just give him time." C.J. hesitated. He looked worried.

"What's wrong?" Stephanie asked.

"Well, I, uh—I really want to help you with Comet as much as I can—" C.J. brushed his hair off his face. "I mean, if we worked with Comet *every* day, maybe he'd catch on quicker."

Stephanie blinked. "I'd love to meet every day, C.J., but I can't. Not because I don't want to, but my sister gets to have Comet on Tuesdays, Thursdays, and weekends. At least for the next week."

"Oh." C.J. looked disappointed. "So you can't bring Comet to the park tomorrow?"

Stephanie shook her head.

"Well, I was wondering . . ." C.J. pushed his hair back again. "Since you don't have Comet on Saturday, do you want to go to the movies with me?"

"Sure." Stephanie grinned. "That would be great." Excellent! Stephanie's hunch about C.J. had been right. He was interested in her. And she was definitely interested in him, too.

"Cool," C.J. cheered. He pulled a stubby pencil and a folded paper from his pocket. He wrote something, then handed the paper to her. "Here's my phone number."

Stephanie reached for the pencil, tore a blank corner off the paper, and scribbled her phone number. "Here's mine."

"Thanks." C.J. stuffed the paper in his pocket with the pencil. He checked his watch. "Oh, man. I've got to go now. But I'll call you. Bye, Stephanie."

"See you here on Friday," Stephanie called after C.J. as he dashed away.

Excellent, Stephanie thought. *One of the coolest guys I've ever met is interested in me! And it's all thanks to . . .*

Stephanie glanced around. Wait a minute. Where was Comet?

She had been so interested in C.J. that she hadn't been keeping an eye on her dog. Now he was gone.

Oh, no! Stephanie started to panic. *I've lost Comet!*

"Comet! Here, boy!" Stephanie's heart pounded as she looked around the field for the dog. Suddenly she caught sight of Cathy. The young woman was walking out of the woods—with Comet and Morrin following behind her. Stephanie sagged with relief.

"I got halfway down the trail and realized I had an extra dog," Cathy called as she approached Stephanie.

"Boy, am I glad to see you." Stephanie hugged Comet and clipped the leash to his collar. "Thanks, Cathy. I thought he was gone."

"No problem. We'll see you soon." Cathy

smiled and waved as she jogged back toward the woods with Morrin.

"Thanks again," Stephanie called. She turned to Comet. "I think we've had enough excitement for one day, boy. Let's go home." She strode toward the park exit.

C.J. definitely likes me! Stephanie thought happily. *And I'm going to see him Friday afternoon at the park* and *Saturday for the movies.*

Comet jerked her to a stop so that he could sniff at something along the sidewalk. *And it's a good thing I'll be seeing so much of C.J.,* Stephanie thought. *If we don't work with Comet, there's no way he can win anything at the dog show.*

Stephanie was *not* going to let Michelle down.

Chapter
8

This is so cool!" Mandy exclaimed when she saw the agility course in the Tanner backyard.

"My dad built it." Michelle beamed with pride.

"Get down, Comet!" Cassie pushed the dog away when he jumped up to greet her and tried to lick her face.

"Comet, heel!" Michelle glared at the dog.

Comet began running in a circle around Michelle and her two best friends.

"Now you know why I asked you guys to come over." Exasperated, Michelle caught Comet's collar and hooked the leash to it. She had been so hopeful when Comet obeyed all her commands on Sunday afternoon. Then he totally lost it on Tuesday and wouldn't even try to do anything.

"What do you want us to do?" Cassie asked.

"Didn't your book say only one person was supposed to train a dog?" Mandy gave Michelle a curious look.

"Yup. I'm the only one who should give him commands. Like for obedience stuff," Michelle explained. "But I need help to teach him what to do on the agility course."

"What should we do?" Mandy asked.

"When I lead him through the obstacles, you guys have to make sure he does them right. He can't go around them or anything."

Cassie nodded. "We can do that."

Mandy wasn't as confident. "Comet won't growl at me or anything, will he?"

"Comet?" Michelle laughed. "Comet never growls at anyone. Unless there's something about them he really doesn't like. He likes you."

As if to prove the point, Comet shoved his nose under Mandy's hand, asking her to pet him.

"See?" Michelle smiled, then tugged on the leash. "Okay, Comet! Time to get to work."

To her surprise, Comet stepped up to her side and sat down. *I hope he's not just tired again*, she thought.

"Heel, Comet!" Michelle walked forward.

Comet pulled back.

"I don't think he wants to go," Cassie said.

"Maybe he doesn't like being ordered around," Mandy suggested. "What happens if you say 'please'?"

"That's not in the book." Disappointed and frustrated, Michelle took a closer look at Comet. He hung his head as if he were unhappy. *That doesn't make sense*, she thought. *He's played at the park with Stephanie more than he's worked with me all week.*

"What's he supposed to do?" Mandy asked.

"Just regular dog stuff." Michelle threw up her arms. "You know, like sit and stay and come and stuff like that."

"That doesn't sound like much fun to me." Cassie leaned over and looked Comet in the eye. "Is that the problem, Comet? Aren't you having any fun?"

Michelle snapped her fingers. "That's it!"

Cassie looked back. "What?"

"Stephanie has been doing all the fun things with Comet and I've just been making him work!"

"Well, the agility course looks like fun," Mandy said.

"Right." Michelle took the leash off Comet's collar and tossed it aside. "You guys get ready, okay?"

"Okay," Cassie said. Mandy nodded.

Comet stood up and shook himself. He looked more excited already.

"Come on, Comet!" Michelle used her "play" voice. Comet always followed when Michelle was playing with him. *Maybe I can trick him into following me up and down the ramp.* "Want to run?"

Michelle ran with Comet bounding after her. However, when she ran up the ramp, across the bridge, and down the other side, Comet ran around it.

"Sorry, Michelle," Cassie called. "You went too fast!"

"Okay. Let's try it again." Michelle called Comet and tried the ramp again. This time Cassie and Mandy positioned themselves on either side of the bridge.

When Comet started to go around again, Cassie grabbed his collar and dragged him back toward the ramp. Mandy picked up his front paws and set them on the plywood.

"Come on, Comet," Michelle coaxed from the top. "It's okay, boy. You can do it."

Mandy pushed him from behind, but the dog just pushed back. "He won't budge."

"Why not try something easier, Michelle?" Cassie looked around. "What about the jumps?"

Michelle was willing to try anything.

Comet wasn't.

Working together, the three girls tried to herd Comet over the jumps. The best they could do was force him to crawl under the plastic pipe. Michelle did manage to lead him around the wastepaper baskets, but he absolutely refused to go into the canvas tunnel.

Michelle finally sank to the ground in disgust. "I don't get it. I thought for sure Comet would like the agility course."

Comet lay down beside her and rested his head in her lap.

"Why should he?" Mandy sat next to the dog and ran her hand over his long fur.

"What do you mean?" Cassie asked. She flopped on her stomach and picked at the grass.

"Well, what does Comet get out of doing all this stuff?" Mandy looked at Cassie, then at Michelle. "I mean, people work at jobs to get money and kids do chores to earn their allowances. What does a dog want?"

"Treats." Michelle sighed.

"Then why aren't you giving him treats?" Cassie asked.

"Well, they count points off for it at the dog show," Michelle explained. "Dogs who do stuff right without getting rewarded get more points. I bet Rachel's dog does everything perfectly without treats."

"Maybe," Mandy agreed. "But Comet doesn't do *anything* without them. It's treats or nothing."

Michelle nodded. Mandy was right. *If I don't bribe Comet with treats, I might as well forget about the dog show*, she thought. *Besides, if I give him treats in practice, at least he'll figure out what he's supposed to do.*

Michelle got a pocket full of moist Beefy-Bites from the kitchen, then joined her friends back outside.

Comet lifted his head, his nose twitching. He jumped up when Michelle slipped her hand into her pocket.

"He knows I've got something," Michelle said. "I sure hope this works."

"Me, too." Mandy stood up and brushed dry grass off her shorts. "I really don't want to listen to Rachel brag about her dog for a month."

"So let's get started." Cassie ran to the ramp.

Michelle pulled a treat out of her pocket and held it up.

Comet sat in front of her with his eyes glued to the treat.

"Want it, Comet?" Michelle asked. "Then come and get it!"

Michelle headed for the two cinder-block jumps and leaped over them.

Comet flew over the plastic pipe, too.

"Good boy!" Michelle gave the dog the Beefy-Bite and made a big fuss over him. Then she pulled another treat out of her pocket. "Ready. Set . . . go!"

Michelle raced for the ramp with Comet on her heels. Cassie and Mandy were in position on either side. When Comet paused at the end of the ramp, Michelle waved the treat.

Comet barked and leaped onto the bridge part instead of running up the ramp. He ran down the other side close behind Michelle. She decided that was good enough and gave him the treat.

"See? Now, that wasn't so bad, was it?" Energized, Michelle lured the dog with a treat as she wove around the wastepaper baskets. He went around only one basket the wrong way.

That's better than nothing! Michelle thought as she headed for the tunnel. She got on her hands and knees and crawled halfway through before she realized Comet wasn't following. She twisted around in the tunnel and held out the treat.

"Come on, boy. This is easy!" Michelle waved the Beefy-Bite in front of his nose.

Comet stuck his head inside the canvas and whined.

"Get ready, Michelle!" Cassie called. "We're gonna push him."

"I'm ready." Michelle inched backward as Cassie and Mandy pushed Comet into the tunnel. Once he was inside, he couldn't wait to get out. He didn't have to crawl like Michelle, though, so he could move a lot faster. She backed out of the tunnel with his cold nose right in her face!

"Yes!" Mandy raised her fists in the air when Michelle and Comet emerged.

Michelle smiled and gave Comet the treat. Although they had gotten him to go around the course, he still had to learn to do it by himself.

In nine short days.

Stephanie and Comet had already left for the park when Michelle got home from school on Friday. Michelle sat on the front steps and stared down the street in the direction of the park. Comet had been so exhausted after doing the agility course the day before that he hadn't even wanted to play with Michelle at all afterward.

Maybe Comet is mad at me because all I make him do is work lately, she thought. *Maybe I should go play with him at the park like Stephanie does.*

Michelle glanced back at the door. Aunt Becky and her dad were still at work. Uncle Jesse and Joey were upstairs, working on a comedy act for a charity event while they watched the twins. She wasn't supposed to go to the park alone. . . .

"No problem." Michelle grinned. *Stephanie is at the park, so I won't be alone when I get there.*

The park was only a few blocks away. Michelle was extra careful crossing the streets. When she got to the park, she followed the signs to the new Canine Play and Run area. She stopped at the end of the baseball field to look for her sister.

Stephanie and Comet were playing under a tree on the far side of the long, grassy meadow. Michelle started running toward her sister. But halfway across the field, she stopped in her tracks and stared.

Stephanie was walking in a large circle, making Comet heel and sit. Then she held her hand out, palm down, and moved it toward the ground. "Down, Comet," Michelle could hear her sister command.

That's all wrong! Michelle thought in horror. *That's not the command to make him lie down. That's the command for "stay."* Michelle had thought Comet was playing all these days at the park. *I didn't think Stephanie was training him.*

Comet wasn't getting any playtime at all! No wonder he never wanted to work.

It's even worse than that, Michelle thought as she started running again. *Stephanie's teaching Comet completely different hand signals from mine.* The first chapter in the dog book had warned her what might happen if Comet had more than one trainer. There were different ways to train a dog, and with two different trainers, the dog would get mixed signals.

Poor Comet is so confused that he doesn't know what to do, Michelle thought. *And there's only a week left before the dog show. Now I'll never get him ready in time.*

Chapter
9

Stephanie!" a voice yelled.

Stephanie stopped and looked around when she heard her name.

"Hi, Michelle!" Stephanie called when she caught sight of her sister running toward her. "What are you doing here?"

Michelle caught her breath, "Looking for you."

"Is something wrong?" Stephanie asked. She couldn't tell if Michelle was angry or upset or both.

"Yes." Michelle was almost in tears. "Why are you training Comet when I *said* I can't have any help?"

77

"'Can't have help?'" Stephanie repeated. "What does that mean? Does the dog show have a rule that you have to train your own dog?"

Comet looked at Stephanie, then at Michelle.

Michelle shook her head. "No, but the training book says a dog should have only *one* trainer so it doesn't get all mixed up by different commands. Which is exactly what you're doing—mixing him up!"

"What did I do?" Stephanie was totally confused.

"You *pointed* to make Comet heel. But I do this"—Michelle patted her leg with her hand—"just like the lady on TV."

Stephanie frowned. "That's not the same signal."

"That's what I'm trying to tell you," Michelle threw up her hands. "You're using different signals, Stephanie. That's *one* reason Comet won't do anything right."

"What's the other reason?" Stephanie asked with a sinking feeling.

Michelle rolled her eyes. "You were supposed to bring Comet to the park so he could have some time to play. Not more time to work."

"Oh, no." Stephanie exhaled. "I'm sorry, Michelle. I didn't know. I, uh—was just watching someone train a dog, and I thought I could help get Comet to behave for you."

"For me?" Michelle took a deep breath and calmed down.

Stephanie decided not to mention that the "someone" was a cute boy named C.J. She really *had* wanted to help, and she didn't want Michelle to think she had been training Comet just to attract a boy.

"I know how much you want Comet to win a ribbon at the dog show, Michelle." Stephanie shrugged. "I was only trying to help."

"I'm sorry I got mad," Michelle apologized. "I'm glad you wanted to help me, but don't do it anymore, okay?"

"Promise." Stephanie handed Michelle Comet's leash.

Comet walked up to Michelle and sniffed her pocket.

"Sorry, boy." Michelle held her hands out. "No treats today."

Comet lay down to pout.

"You give him treats when you're training

him?" Stephanie asked. C.J. had told her not to do that. "Is that a good idea?"

"It is when you have a dog who won't work for nothing." Michelle shrugged. "The book said that, too."

"Well, if the book said it, it must be right." Stephanie felt bad about confusing Comet with different hand signals. She wasn't going to argue with Michelle about the book. C.J. had done a great job of training Jasper, but training Comet was Michelle's project.

Where is C.J., anyway? Stephanie wondered. She looked across the meadow, but there was no sign of him.

"Would you walk me home now, Stephanie?" Michelle asked. "I think Comet needs a day off."

"Sure." Stephanie was disappointed, but she didn't want to stay at the park by herself if C.J. wasn't going to show. Cathy wasn't even there so Comet could play with Morrin. She looked back one more time as she followed Michelle and Comet toward the baseball field.

I just hope C.J. calls or shows up at the movies tomorrow, she thought.

*   *   *

Stephanie helped Aunt Becky unhook the twins from their toddler seats in the mall parking lot. As soon as she and Michelle had arrived home, Aunt Becky invited them to go shopping with her. She wanted to get the boys new clothes, but she needed someone to keep an eye on them while she got a haircut.

"Where is Darcy meeting us?" Aunt Becky asked. She took Nicky by the hand.

"In the center courtyard," Stephanie said. Michelle had decided to stay home and brush Comet, so Stephanie had invited Darcy. Allie couldn't come because she had another date with Chris.

"Don't run ahead, Alex," Aunt Becky said.

"Not so fast!" Stephanie laughed and playfully grabbed Alex before he ran across the parking lot.

Alex giggled and gave Stephanie his hand.

When they got into the mall, they spotted Darcy right away. She ran over to them. "Hi!"

"Hi, Darcy." Aunt Becky grinned. "Have you been waiting long?"

"We're a little late because we couldn't find Alex's right shoe," Stephanie explained.

"That's okay. I've been here only a few minutes." Darcy looked down when Nicky tugged on her hand.

"Do you like ice cream?" Nicky asked Darcy.

"Only when my mother says it's okay." Darcy looked at Aunt Becky and took Nicky's hand. "Where to first?"

"Well—" Aunt Becky shifted her gaze between Stephanie and Darcy. "How about you two keep these little cowboys occupied while I relax for thirty minutes in the beauty salon?"

"I think we can handle that." Stephanie actually enjoyed watching the twins, but she could almost feel her aunt's relief as she smiled and walked away.

"Let's go to the toy store," Nicky cried. "Please!"

"Yeah! Toy store!" Alex yelled, jumping up and down.

"Okay, but only if you're quiet and stop jumping," Stephanie said.

"Are they this enthusiastic all the time?" Darcy asked as the boys pulled them toward the toy store.

"Except when they're asleep!" Stephanie

laughed. "So have you met Allie's new boyfriend yet?"

"No." Darcy shook her head. "Have you?"

"No. I haven't even seen a picture," Stephanie said. "I'm just glad she found someone she really likes who likes her back."

"Me, too." Darcy nodded. "I'd love to meet someone as cool as Chris seems to be. Even if he doesn't go to our school."

"Well . . . I think I did," Stephanie blurted out.

"You did?" Darcy's head snapped around. "Who? Where?"

"Would you believe at the park?" Stephanie had been dying to talk to someone about C.J. and couldn't wait to tell Darcy everything. "His name is C.J. and he's absolutely terrific. Just like Allie's new boyfriend!"

"Cute, nice, and cool, huh?" Darcy grinned.

"Completely," Stephanie said. "We're going to the movies tomorrow afternoon."

"Maybe you and C.J. should double-date with Chris and Allie," Darcy suggested. "Chris and C.J. sound so much alike, they're sure to get along with each other."

"That's a great idea." Stephanie looked down when Alex yanked her to a halt.

"We're here." Alex laughed. "You weren't paying attention."

Stephanie smiled. "You're right. Come on!"

The boys tugged Stephanie and Darcy up and down the aisles, pulling toys off the shelves to examine them. The girls couldn't put things back as fast as the twins took them down.

Nicky spotted the remote-controlled cars on a shelf beyond his reach. "Can I see that, Stephanie?"

"Just for a minute." Stephanie stood on tiptoe to reach the sleek black and silver Tornado Thunder box. "No touching. Just look."

Alex's and Nicky's eyes shone as they stared at the turbocharged, battery driven, remote-controlled car.

"Cool," Alex said.

"Can we make it go?" Nicky asked.

"No, we can't because it isn't ours," Stephanie explained.

Both boys seemed so disappointed, Stephanie decided to give them a special treat. She knew the twins loved the little riding machines scattered around the mall. She even had some quarters in her purse. "How about rides?"

"The fire truck," Alex cried.

"I want the spaceship," Nicky said.

"You got it. Let's go!" Stephanie and Darcy latched on to the boys and hurried out of the store.

"We're in luck," Stephanie told Darcy as they started back toward the central dome. "The fire truck and the spaceship are in the same spot."

Four rides were grouped in an alcove off the main concourse. Stephanie was relieved to see that nobody else was using them when they arrived. Nicky climbed right into the spaceship, but Alex hesitated.

Stephanie found several quarters in the bottom of her purse and gave some to Darcy. "Don't you want the fire truck now, Alex?"

"Yeah, but I need to go to the bathroom." Alex started to jiggle up and down.

"Okay." Stephanie glanced at Darcy. "I'd better get Alex to the rest room. Do you want to wait for us here?"

"Sure. The closest one is by the Game Arcade." Darcy slipped two quarters into the ride slot as Stephanie rushed away with Alex in tow.

After Alex used the rest room, Stephanie took his hand and started back toward the rides.

"Look, Stephanie. It's Allie," Alex said loudly. Stephanie looked where her cousin was pointing. Sure enough, Allie was standing near the mall door.

She had her arms around a boy!

So that's her new boyfriend, Stephanie thought. She couldn't see the boy's face, but his dark hair looked nice. *I don't want to interrupt Allie when she's on a date,* Stephanie thought. *But maybe I'll just hang around until I can get a look at Chris. Darcy will be dying to know what he looks like.*

Stephanie pulled Alex behind a planter and put her fingers to her lips to keep the boy quiet.

"Are we playing hide-and-seek with Allie?" Alex whispered.

Stephanie nodded. "I want to look at Allie's friend, and then we have to go tell Darcy what he's like," she explained. "It's a game."

She peeked around the planter and watched as Allie and Chris joined hands and walked in their direction. As they got closer, Stephanie got a good look at Chris's face.

Wait a minute, she thought. She leaned out from behind the plant and took another peek.

This can't be happening, she thought. *My eyes must be playing tricks on me.*

Stephanie ducked back behind the planter as Allie and Chris walked by.

"This is awful," Stephanie moaned as the horrible truth sank in. "Allie's boyfriend, Chris, is C.J.!"

Chapter
10

After breakfast on Saturday, Michelle ran back upstairs to look for Comet. She almost ran right into her oldest sister. D.J. was in college and didn't spend much time at home anymore.

"Careful, Michelle!" D.J. grabbed the banister. "What's the rush?"

"The dog show is a week from today!" Michelle kept on going to the second floor.

Michelle wanted to get an early start so Comet could have *two* training sessions today. *Obedience and tricks this morning, then agility this afternoon.* Training the dog would be hard, though. Stephanie had been trying to help, but now Comet had all his signals confused. She didn't have any time to waste.

Except I have to find Comet first!

Michelle skidded to a stop outside the bedroom she shared with Stephanie when she heard Stephanie talking on the phone.

"Yeah, I'm really"—Stephanie coughed—"sorry, C.J., but—" She coughed again—twice! "I'm too sick to go to the movies today." *Cough, cough.*

Michelle peeked in the door. She knew Stephanie wasn't sick. She didn't cough once during breakfast!

"No, I'll probably be sick on Monday, too." *Cough, cough.* Stephanie turned and saw Michelle. She waved her inside and rolled her eyes. "I might be sick all week." *Cough.* "Bye!"

"What was that all about?" Michelle didn't want to pry, but she was too curious not to ask. Comet was lying on the floor between the two beds. She stepped around him and hopped onto her bed.

Stephanie sighed as she hung up. "Just some guy who isn't as cool as I thought he was."

"Really?" Michelle asked.

"Yeah." Stephanie leaned back against the wall. "I don't want to see him anymore, so I won't be taking Comet back to the park for a while."

Ah-ha! Michelle smiled. *Now I know the real reason Stephanie wanted to go to the park with Comet. A boy!* She didn't say anything, though. Stephanie looked really depressed.

Michelle felt bad that she was secretly glad this boy was out of the picture. *Now I can train Comet* every *day until the show.*

"It's too bad for Comet, though," Stephanie added. "He really liked playing with this yellow Lab named Morrin at the park."

"Well, after the dog show, we can both take Comet to the park to play," Michelle suggested.

Stephanie smiled. "By then I think C.J. will have gotten the message. Not interested."

"I've got to get to work," Michelle slipped off the bed and shook the sleeping dog. "Come on, Comet! Let's go!"

Comet stood up and shook his gleaming golden fur.

"His coat is really starting to shine, Michelle." Stephanie nodded with approval.

"I brushed him for hours yesterday!" Michelle rubbed her arm. "But after I groom him I have to lock him in the house or he rolls in the dirtiest spot he can find. It's going to be a long week."

Stephanie sighed. "That's for sure."

On Sunday morning Danny stopped Michelle on her way outside for Comet's first training session. "Why don't you give Comet a break this morning, Michelle?"

"Well . . ." Michelle was starting to feel a little frantic. Yesterday afternoon Comet totally refused to go through the tunnel. He also thought it was more fun to run *under* the bridge part of the ramp than to go over it.

"There's something I want you to see," her dad insisted.

"Okay. What is it?"

"You'll see. Come on." Danny pulled his keys out of his pocket and walked Michelle to the car.

Michelle felt excited as she climbed into the front seat. "Where are we going?"

"Anderson's Dog Training School." Danny grinned. "I'm impressed with how hard you've been working with Comet. I thought it might help to watch how the professionals do it. You might pick up some pointers."

"Cool!" Michelle settled back against the seat. Her father was really interested in what she was doing. The whole family was. *I can't let them down now. Comet just has to win a blue ribbon. Even if it's only in the biscuit-catching class.*

That was the one thing Comet was doing better, Michelle thought as they drove into the country. Lately he was catching one out of two biscuits instead of one out of three.

At Anderson's Danny led the way to where obedience classes were taking place. He and Michelle sat down on folding chairs along the wall to watch. "Those must be beginners," Danny said.

Michelle looked to the left and nodded. Ten frustrated men and women were trying to get their dogs to "stay." All of the dogs kept getting up. Some of them ran to their owners. Others ran to meet other dogs. Everyone looked tense even though the instructor was calm and encouraging.

Michelle knew exactly how they felt.

"Does all that look familiar?" Danny asked.

"Yep." Michelle nodded. "I have the same problem with Comet."

Danny smiled and pointed to the right. "Well, if you stick with it, one day Comet will obey like those dogs."

Michelle's mouth fell open as she watched the dogs on the right. None of them were on a leash, and some of the people did use treats. But not all, Michelle noticed. The dogs walked right by their owners' sides no matter how many quick turns they made. When the instructor told them to make the dogs "stand" and "stay," all the people left the ring and went into the training store. All the dogs stood like statues, staring at the store door, waiting.

"Pretty impressive, huh?" Danny grinned.

"I'll say!" Michelle was impressed and dismayed. She couldn't imagine that Comet would ever be *that* well trained, but her dad obviously thought she could do it. *It's a good thing the*

Children's Dog Show has beginner classes or I'd be completely out of luck.

"Can we go watch the agility stuff?" Michelle asked.

"Yeah, all that running and jumping is probably more exciting." Danny stood up and led her back outside.

As they turned the corner at the end of the building, Michelle stopped dead. "Wow! Look at that!"

"What?" Danny paused with a puzzled frown.

The training center supply store was attached to the end of the large building. Several doghouses of different styles and sizes were on display outside.

Michelle ran up to a large wooden doghouse with real shingles on the roof. She leaned over to look inside. "This one even has a floor and a pad!"

"Don't you like your room anymore?" Danny teased.

"I don't want it for me." Michelle giggled. "For Comet!"

"Oh, for Comet." Danny took a moment to

inspect the doghouse, then nodded. "Well, it's a great doghouse, but I'll have to think about it, okay?"

"Okay." Michelle looked back as she followed her dad toward the white fence around one of the agility courses. *Comet would love that doghouse*, she thought. *I just know it.*

"Now, *that's* an agility course," Danny said, stopping by the fence.

The course was similar to the one pictured in the library book, but that wasn't what grabbed Michelle's attention.

Rachel was standing with a group of people at the far end of the course. A dog that looked like a miniature collie with long, silky brown-and-white fur sat by her side. *That must be Bonnie Blue,* Michelle thought. She was sure Bonnie Blue never rolled in a compost heap.

"Wow, this is great!" Danny's eyes lit up as a black Lab sped through the course. A man guided the dog with hand and voice commands. "Look at him go!"

Michelle was looking. The man moved his arm in a sweeping gesture toward an obstacle that had steps instead of a ramp. The dog trotted up, over, and down without hesitation. All the man did was point at the tunnel, and the dog whipped through it. The Lab leaped over the jumps and wound in and around a line of white cones.

"I can understand why you wanted to teach Comet agility, Michelle," Danny said. "Those dogs are amazing."

Yeah, they sure are, Michelle thought as Rachel and Bonnie Blue ran the course in the same patterns. Bonnie Blue didn't do the course as perfectly as the black Lab.

But compared to Comet, Bonnie Blue is a genius, Michelle thought.

Instead of feeling more confident, Michelle felt worse now that she knew what professionally trained dogs could do. *But I can't tell Dad that*, Michelle thought. *He's only trying to help me. Just like Stephanie.*

When the agility class ended, Michelle followed Danny into the ring. Her father wanted to take a closer look at the course.

"Hi, Michelle," Rachel called out.

"Hi, Rachel." Michelle smiled and hung back while Danny went to look at the ramp.

Bonnie Blue walked quietly on Rachel's left side and sat when Rachel stopped in front of Michelle.

Rachel didn't even have to say sit, Michelle realized.

"Are you signing up for lessons with Comet?" Rachel asked.

"No, I'm training him myself at home," Michelle said. "We have our own agility course."

"Oh, but you just *started* training Comet, right?" Rachel cocked her head. "You know it takes months to teach a dog how to do agility, don't you?"

"Comet is learning really fast," Michelle said. *And he is,* she thought, *for a beginner.*

"Not even a *professional* can train a good agility dog in two weeks, Michelle." Rachel shifted her gaze. "Oh, there's my dad. I have to go."

"See you tomorrow at school, Rachel."

As Rachel walked away, Bonnie Blue heeled without being told. Rachel looked back and smiled. "Isn't Bonnie great?"

"Yeah, she's super." Michelle waved, then

sighed. *I'll just have to work harder with Comet all week,* she thought. Comet just had to win a blue ribbon so her family would be proud of her.

"And so Rachel can't tell everyone in our class that I'm a loser," Michelle muttered.

Chapter
11

"Chris called me when his family plans got changed on Saturday, so we went to the movies," Allie said at lunch on Wednesday. "I just can't believe how lucky I am. I mean, he's such a great guy."

Stephanie lowered her eyes to the table. This was terrible. What was she supposed to do?

"When are we going to meet him?" Darcy asked.

The *last* thing Stephanie wanted was to meet Chris. *Or C.J. depending on what girl he's going out with,* she thought, fuming. He hadn't known Allie was Stephanie's best friend, but that didn't change anything. He had still asked her for a date when he was already going out with someone else. Chris was a no-good cheater. *And because of him, I almost betrayed my best friend.*

"Well, I don't know." Allie paused.

When nobody said anything for a minute, Stephanie looked up. Allie and Darcy were both staring at her.

"Okay, Stephanie." Darcy put her fork down. "I can't stand it anymore. What's wrong?"

"Wrong?" Stephanie faked a look of surprise. "Nothing. Why?"

"You've been acting kind of weird all week," Allie said. "And when you get real quiet, it usually means that something's wrong."

"Right." Darcy leaned forward. "And whatever it is, it can't be so bad you can't tell us."

Allie nodded. "We might be able to help."

I doubt it, Stephanie thought. Allie was so happy with Chris. How could Stephanie tell her that her great new boyfriend was a two-timer? *Or that he almost two-timed her with me.* She couldn't even tell Darcy, because Darcy might tell Allie—if she thought it was the right thing to do.

"Did you break up with C.J.?" Darcy asked.

"Who's C.J.?" Allie asked.

If only you knew, Stephanie thought desperately.

Darcy started to answer. "This cute guy Stephanie met—"

"But it didn't work out," Stephanie interrupted. She had been so upset about finding out that C.J. was Allie's boyfriend that she forgot she told Darcy about meeting him. "He, uh— wasn't as cool as I thought."

"That's too bad," Darcy said.

"Guess that's why you didn't tell me about him, huh?" Allie asked.

Stephanie nodded. "There wasn't much point." She was so confused. She didn't like hiding the truth from Allie, but she didn't want to be responsible for Allie's broken heart, either. Joey had always said, "When in doubt, do nothing."

Right now that seemed like good advice.

"Well, it's probably a good thing you found out C.J. wasn't as great as you thought before you went out with him, Stephanie." Darcy's forehead wrinkled with a frown. "It's still a bummer, though."

"Yeah," Allie said. "No wonder you feel so down."

"Well, actually—I'm really worried about Michelle," Stephanie said. She had to change the subject or they would never stop talking about C.J. "She's been working so hard training Comet for the dog show, and I almost totally ruined everything."

"How?" Darcy asked.

Stephanie frowned. "She couldn't get Comet to do what she tells him, so I tried training him on my own to help her out."

"What's wrong with that?" Allie asked.

"I was using different signals from Michelle's, and poor Comet got so confused that he went on strike and wouldn't do anything."

"Poor Michelle." Allie took a sip of milk.

"Yeah." Stephanie sighed. "She wants Comet to win a blue ribbon so much, but I don't think he has a chance."

Allie set her milk carton down and grinned. "I have a great idea. Maybe Chris could help her."

"What?" Stephanie yelped. Her head spun. This was *not* good!

"Yeah." Allie's eyes lit up with enthusiasm.

"Chris has been training his dog over at Anderson's Dog Training School for a long time. He knows all about this kind of stuff."

"Do you think he would?" Darcy asked. "Help Michelle with Comet, I mean."

"No. Not a good idea," Stephanie blurted out. There was no way she could deal with seeing Chris and having to pretend she didn't know him. *Besides, I don't know what Chris might say or do*, she thought.

"Why not?" Darcy asked. She looked as confused as Comet.

"Because . . . well . . . Michelle wants to do it herself," Stephanie quickly explained. "If Comet does win something, it won't mean anything unless Michelle can take the credit."

"Oh, well, I guess that makes sense," Allie said.

"It really does," Stephanie agreed. "She's even got a book that says a dog should have only one trainer."

"Okay." Allie jabbed a french fry with her fork.

"Thanks anyway." Stephanie smiled. *Whew! That would have been a major crisis.*

"You know," Allie pushed her tray aside and folded her arms on the table. "I'm going to that dog show with Chris this weekend. He's entering his dog, Jasper."

"He is?" Stephanie withered inside. She should have realized that. Jasper was too well trained *not* to enter.

"If Michelle is having trouble with Comet, I bet Chris would help her at the dog show," Allie said. "We could all hang out together. You, me, and Chris!"

"I'll, uh—remember that." Now Stephanie really didn't know what to do.

She had promised Michelle she'd go to the dog show with Joey and their dad to cheer her and Comet on. She couldn't stay home and hurt her sister's feelings.

If Chris was there with her best friend, though, there was no way she could avoid him.

Should I just pretend I don't know him and hope he does the same thing?

Or should I tell Allie that her wonderful boyfriend is really a two-timing loser—and that I know because he tried to go out with me?

Chapter
12

$\mathbb{F}$riday evening Michelle got everything ready in the bathroom before she brought Comet in to take a bath. *The only thing Comet hates worse than taking a bath is going to the vet*, she thought as she got a pile of clean towels out of the linen closet. Joey had just done the laundry and there were plenty.

Michelle put the towels on the hamper. Then she set the dog shampoo on the floor by the tub with an empty plastic bowl. He was a big dog and she would have to pour water over him to get all the shampoo suds out of his fur. When everything was ready, she went downstairs to get the dog.

1 0 5

Joey was in the kitchen, finishing the dishes. "So tomorrow's the big day."

"Yeah." Michelle got the leash out of the junk drawer. "Are you still coming?"

"Are you kidding?" Joey flipped the dishtowel over his shoulder. "Nothing could keep me away from your dog-show debut."

"Good." Michelle sighed. "Because I'm going to be really nervous."

"That's normal." Joey gave her a quick hug. "Everybody gets stage fright. Even me, sometimes. But you're doing something really great, Michelle. Just remember that."

"Thanks, Joey." Michelle smiled. She still had butterflies in her stomach, but she felt better. When she had decided to enter the dog show, she hadn't really thought about all the people who would be there watching. "Have you seen Comet?"

"Under the table." Joey pointed and whispered.

"Oh." Michelle whispered back and tiptoed over. She leaned down, grabbed Comet by the collar, and clipped on the leash. She pulled, but the dog refused to come. "I think he knows I'm going to give him a you-know-what."

"Probably. Want some help?" Joey held out his hand.

"Please." Michelle handed him the leash.

"Becky and Jesse are bringing the twins down for ice cream in a little while. Do you want some?" Joey got down on his hands and knees and dragged Comet out from under the table.

"Sure," Michelle said. "But not until after I finish Comet's bath."

Michelle went upstairs first, but she didn't turn on the water. She waited until Joey got Comet into the bathroom and closed the door behind him when he left. The dog dropped down onto the floor and stared at her with worried eyes.

"Don't look at me like that, Comet." Michelle unclipped the leash and took off his collar. She set them both on the sink counter. "You'll be a clean, happy puppy when this is over."

Michelle had put on old clothes because she knew she was going to get wet and dirty. When it came to baths, Comet was even less cooperative than he was during training. She had to push him over to the tub. Then she struggled to lift his front legs over the rim. The dog didn't fight her, but he didn't help her, either. When she finally got him inside the tub, she turned on the water. She made sure it wasn't too hot or too cold before she put in the drain stopper.

"Don't be sad, Comet." Michelle talked as she poured clean water over him with the plastic bowl. "You did a lot better in training today."

Sort of, Michelle thought. She didn't want to wear him out the night before the big show, so she had gone over everything only once. He still didn't know all the obedience commands, but he knew some. He wouldn't run the agility course by himself, but he hardly ever missed catching a biscuit.

"I'll make you a promise, Comet." Michelle squirted dog shampoo all over his golden fur, then rubbed it into a lather. "If you win a blue ribbon tomorrow, I'll get you one of those big rawhide bones."

Comet whined.

"Okay. I'll get you one of those big rawhide bones even if you don't win. I guess you *have* earned it."

It seemed to take forever to rinse out all the shampoo. When Michelle finished, the water was brown with dirt. As she reached for a towel, Comet leaped out of the tub and started to shake.

"Wait, Comet!" Michelle threw a towel over him to stop the water from getting all over everything. She got most of the water out of his thick coat by rubbing him with towels, but she couldn't get him completely dry. When she looked in the sink cabinet for the hair dryer, it wasn't there.

"Wait here, Comet. I'll be right back." Michelle pulled the bathroom door closed and went to her room. Stephanie liked to sit on her bed and dry her hair. Michelle searched their room for the hair dryer, but she didn't see it anywhere. Finally she found it stuffed in the closet.

Poor Comet must be getting lonely. Michelle grinned, picturing the big, wet retriever stuck in the bathroom. He certainly was a patient dog.

When Michelle stepped out into the hallway, she saw that the bathroom door was open—and Comet wasn't inside.

"Oh, boy," Michelle muttered. *If Comet gets wet paw prints all over the kitchen floor, Dad will kill me. And if he gets out of the house, he'll go right to Aunt Becky's compost heap to roll in the dirt.*

Michelle couldn't decide which was worse.

Stephanie was coming up the stairs. She stopped in the hall when she saw Michelle's worried face. "What's the matter?" she asked.

"Have you seen Comet?" Michelle was frantic. She really didn't want to give the dog *another* bath.

Stephanie shook her head. "I thought you were giving him a bath."

"I was!" Michelle ran down the stairs and found Aunt Becky and Uncle Jesse in the living room with Nicky.

"Alex? Where are you?" Aunt Becky called, glancing around the room in search of her other son.

"What have you been doing, Michelle?" Uncle Jesse asked. "You're all wet."

"Giving Comet a bath. Have you seen him?" Michelle paused at the bottom of the stairs— and saw Alex standing by the open front door.

"There you are, Alex! Why is the door open?" Aunt Becky asked, coming out of the living room.

"Comet wanted to go out," Alex said.

Oh, no! Michelle raced to the front door and flipped on the porch light. Comet wasn't lying on the porch or sniffing around the front yard. He wasn't in the driveway or on the sidewalk. He wasn't even in the street in front of their house. She didn't see him *anywhere.*

Comet was gone!

Chapter
13

Let's not panic," Danny said. "I'm sure Comet didn't go far."

"This is all my fault." Michelle wiped a tear off her cheek. Everyone was seated around the kitchen table for an emergency family meeting—except Aunt Becky and the twins. Nobody wanted Alex to feel bad because he opened the door for Comet.

"It's not your fault." Stephanie patted Michelle's back to comfort her.

"Yes, it is," Michelle insisted. "I made Comet work all the time and then I gave him a bath. He *hates* baths. That's why he ran away."

"Nobody blames you, Michelle," Danny said. "You shouldn't blame yourself, either. We don't know why Comet . . . left."

"Your dad's right." Joey gave her a tight smile. "You don't blame Alex, do you?"

Michelle shook her head and blinked back another tear. Alex was only four. He didn't know any better.

"Well, I don't care about the dog show or winning a ribbon or anything anymore," Michelle told her family. "I just want to find him and give him a hug."

"What's the plan?" Uncle Jesse asked Danny.

"Well, Becky can stay by the phone," Danny said. "If Animal Control picks him up, they'll look up his license number and call."

Michelle gasped. "No, they can't. I took Comet's collar off when I gave him a bath!"

"Not a problem," Danny quickly interjected. "If Animal Control finds him, he'll spend the night at the pound, but we can go get him in the morning. In the meantime let's search the neighborhood in teams."

"I'll go solo on my motorcycle." Uncle Jesse

stood up. "I can cover more ground faster that way."

"Good idea." Danny pointed to Joey and Stephanie. "You two search the south side. Michelle and I will go north."

"We're on it." Joey jumped up and waved for Stephanie to follow. "Let's move out."

"Wait! It's dark out there. You might need these." Danny reached into the cabinet under the kitchen sink and pulled out three flashlights. He kept the batteries fresh just in case the electricity went out. He tossed one to Uncle Jesse, one to Joey, and palmed the third. "Come on, Michelle. We'll find him."

Michelle held her father's hand as they headed north on the sidewalk. They both called Comet's name, and her father stopped at several houses to ask if anyone had seen the runaway retriever. No one had.

The later it became, the worse Michelle felt. They spent two hours going door-to-door around the neighborhood.

There was no sign of Comet.

Finally her father said it was getting too late and they had to quit for the night.

Joey, Stephanie, and Uncle Jesse were waiting when they got back home.

"Any luck?" Joey asked.

Danny shook his head. "There's nothing else we can do tonight. I suppose we should hope he's at the pound. It's not home, but he'll be safe."

"We'd better all get some sleep so we can call the pound first thing in the morning." Uncle Jesse squeezed Michelle's shoulder as he turned to head upstairs. "Don't worry. We'll find him."

"Come on, Michelle." Stephanie put her arm around Michelle and guided her toward the stairs. "The sooner we get to bed, the sooner we can get up and start searching again. I'll even call Allie and Darcy tomorrow to see if they'll come over to help."

Michelle just nodded. Everyone was being so nice and understanding. But all she could think about was Comet—lost and alone in the dark.

Chapter
14

Stephanie was up at sunrise and on the phone to Darcy. She apologized for calling so early, but when she explained about the missing dog, Darcy understood.

When she went back into her bedroom, Michelle was awake. "Are they coming to help?" Michelle asked, rubbing her eyes. Stephanie noticed they were still red from crying about Comet.

"They sure are. Darcy's going to call Allie, and her mother offered to drive them both here." Stephanie smiled. "We'll have a whole team ready to search the city for Comet."

She wasn't sure whom she was worried about more, Comet or Michelle. She knew her little sister hadn't done anything wrong, but there was nothing she could say to make Michelle stop feeling guilty.

"When can we call the pound?" Michelle slipped out of bed. She had slept in her clothes.

Stephanie glanced at her bedside alarm clock. "Not until eight o'clock," she said. "So you've got plenty of time to get cleaned up and change. I'll go downstairs and help Joey make breakfast."

"I don't think I can eat." Michelle folded her arms around her waist. "My stomach hurts."

"You'll feel better after a shower." Stephanie paused at the door. "And stop worrying. We'll find him. I promise."

As she hurried downstairs, she wished that she could feel as confident as she sounded. Comet had never been gone all night before. Stephanie had no idea what could have happened to him.

Everyone ate a quick breakfast of cereal and juice. Stephanie watched the clock while her father outlined the search plan for the morning. *Only ten minutes to go before the pound opens*, she thought. *And if Comet is there, we can even get him in time for Michelle to make the dog show!*

"I printed these fliers this morning," Joey said. He set a stack of papers on the table. The flier had a picture of Comet that Danny had stored on the hard drive on his computer, along with Comet's name and the Tanners' address and phone number. He pulled two plastic boxes filled with thumbtacks out of the junk drawer. "We can hang them up and search at the same time."

"Good idea," Danny told him. Stephanie saw him glance at Michelle. She had hardly spoken all morning. Stephanie could tell her dad was worried about Michelle, too.

The only thing that will make Michelle feel better is finding Comet, Stephanie thought.

Her eyes darted back to the clock. "It's eight o'clock. Who's going to call the pound?"

"I will. I've got the number right here." Joey held up a slip of paper and went to the wall phone. He described Comet to the person on the other end of the line and rattled off the Tanner phone number. Then he hung up and sighed. "He's not there, but they'll keep a look out."

When the doorbell rang, Stephanie sprang up from her chair. "That's probably Darcy and Allie!"

Stephanie flew into the living room and threw open the door. "Hi, guys. Boy, am I glad to see . . . you." The last word stuck in her throat when she realized that Darcy and Allie were not alone.

Chris and Jasper had come with them!

This cannot be happening, Stephanie thought, stunned.

"Hi, Steph." Allie walked in and gave her a hug. "I'm so sorry about Comet!"

Stephanie caught Chris's eye and glared at him.

Chris smiled, then blinked. He turned pale when he recognized her.

Luckily, everyone else seemed totally unaware that anything was wrong. In fact, Darcy was winking at Stephanie and gesturing for her to check out Allie's boyfriend.

"Stephanie, this is Allie's . . . *friend*, Chris," Darcy said. "He's going to help us search."

Chris cleared his throat and stepped forward with his hands jammed in his pockets. "Uh, hi, Stephanie."

"Hello, *Chris*." Stephanie managed a tight smile. However, she was caught completely off guard when Jasper suddenly sprang toward her as if she were an old friend.

Which I am, Stephanie thought as she petted the excited dog.

"That's strange," Allie said. "Jasper is usually shy around strangers. I've met him several times and he doesn't greet *me* like that."

Stephanie pushed the dog away. "Dogs just like me, I guess," she said lamely.

"Or maybe he smells Comet's scent," Chris added. "On your clothes."

"Oh, right. That's probably it."

Danny came to the door with Michelle. "Hi, kids. You're just in time. I've got everyone assigned to teams. We'll split the neighborhood—"

"Oh, no!" Chris slapped his forehead. "I'm sorry, but I can't stay."

"Why not?" Allie asked.

"I, uh—have something I have to do," Chris said. "For the dog show. I feel really bad about this, but I've got to go. Come, Jasper!"

Chris was down the steps and jogging toward

the sidewalk before anyone could ask any questions.

Allie looked upset, but she tried to cover for him. "Whatever it is, I know it must be really important."

"I'm sure." Stephanie relaxed, totally relieved that Chris was gone. *At least now I can concentrate on finding Comet without worrying about saying or doing something that might hurt Allie.*

"Who was that guy?" Michelle asked.

"A friend of Allie's," Stephanie explained. She quickly diverted everyone's attention. "Okay, Dad. Who's on what team and where do we go?"

Danny quickly read off the assignments. Uncle Jesse had already left on his motorcycle. Aunt Becky would call in a "lost dog" ad when the newspaper office opened. Then she would stay by the phone in case the pound called—or anyone else who had found Comet. Everyone agreed to meet back at the house in two hours.

Darcy and Allie left with Danny's hand-drawn map, a card full of thumbtacks, and a bunch of fliers. Michelle and Joey formed the second team and left with the same supplies. Stephanie went with her father. He turned on his cell phone and put it in his pocket so Aunt Becky could call if there was news.

"You don't think anything bad happened to Comet, do you, Dad?" Stephanie asked as she waited for a car to pass at the first intersection.

"No, I don't," Danny said. "We'll find him and he'll be all right. Tired and hungry, maybe, but safe and sound."

Stephanie nodded, but her dad's positive attitude didn't fool her for a minute. He loved Comet, but he was more concerned about Michelle. *He's putting on a brave face so I don't worry*, she realized. Besides, if they didn't find the dog, her little sister would never forgive herself.

"That's what I think, too, Dad."

Stephanie's confidence didn't last. She and her father searched streets and alleys, tacked up fliers, and talked to everyone they saw for an hour and a half, with no luck. She was fighting back tears by the time Danny put up the last flier in their stash.

Comet had disappeared without a trace.

"Maybe someone else found him and Becky just got so excited she forgot to call." Danny pulled his cell phone out and wandered a short distance away as he dialed.

Worn out, Stephanie sat down and leaned against a tree trunk. She just couldn't believe Comet was gone. In fact, it was hard to believe he had run away in the first place.

The more Stephanie thought about it, the less sense it made. Sure, Comet had gotten a bath and lots of training for the dog show—but it wasn't the first time Michelle had made him do things he didn't like. He hadn't been thrilled when Michelle dressed him in her clothes when she was six or given him a haircut when she was seven.

He didn't run away then, Stephanie thought. *So why did he run away now?*

A dog barked nearby.

"Comet?" Stephanie jumped up to look for her dog. Instead, she saw a small boy playing with a large yellow dog in his front yard. Disappointed, she sat back down.

Watching the happy yellow dog reminded Stephanie of how much Comet liked to play . . . especially with other dogs. He really loved playing with . . . Stephanie blinked. *Wait a minute!*

Danny trudged over, his expression grim.

"Everyone's back at the house, but nobody found him."

"Wait—I think I know where he could be, Dad! Come on!"

Stephanie didn't dare let herself believe that she might be right—just in case she wasn't. She couldn't help thinking, *Please, please, please!* She turned into the park and broke into a jog by the baseball field.

"Stephanie!" a woman's voice called out. "He's over here!"

"Well, I'll be—" A wide grin broke out on her father's face.

Stephanie sighed with relief when she saw Comet sitting with Cathy and Morrin on their usual bench. Comet barked, along with his yellow Lab pal. Cathy waved.

"How did you know, Stephanie?" Danny asked.

"A lucky guess." Stephanie was so relieved that her knees felt weak as she followed her father across the grass.

Comet was so happy to see them that he jumped up and down, pulling on the leash Cathy had slipped around his neck.

Stephanie rushed forward and threw her arms around the dog. She squeezed him until he grunted, then sat back to look him sternly in the eye. "Comet! We've been looking for you everywhere!"

"I was hoping you'd think to come looking in the park," Cathy said after she introduced herself to Danny. "I was out for a late run last night and Comet followed me home. But he didn't have his collar on and I didn't know your last name, so I couldn't call."

They spent a few minutes thanking Cathy, then started back home. Danny got out his cell phone to call with the good news, but his batteries had gone dead.

"I guess I was so worried about Comet last night, I forgot to charge them."

Stephanie was actually kind of glad, because now she wouldn't miss the look on Michelle's face when Comet returned safe and sound. *And she can still get to the dog show this afternoon.*

It looked as if Michelle was in the clear. Unfortunately, all of Stephanie's problems weren't solved yet. Now that she wasn't worried about the dog, she started worrying about Allie. She had decided not to tell Allie about C.J.'s asking her out. But she just couldn't stand to watch him make a fool of her best friend!

Somehow, I have to convince Allie that Chris isn't the great guy she thinks he is, Stephanie decided. *Even if it means that I have to tell her he asked me out.*

She just hoped Allie wouldn't be so upset that she blamed Stephanie.

That was a chance she had to take. *Allie is my best friend and I have to tell her the truth,* Stephanie thought. *Even if it ruins our friendship forever.*

Chapter
15

"This is the worst day of my life." Michelle sat on the front steps with Cassie and Mandy. Aunt Becky had called and asked them to come over. Her aunt thought having her two best friends around might cheer her up. *But they're almost as depressed as I am,* Michelle thought.

"Yeah." Mandy nodded and caught her lower lip with her teeth.

Cassie didn't say anything. Michelle could tell that they were both afraid they might cry if they tried to talk.

And Comet isn't even their dog.

Michelle sighed. She felt all cried out.

127

Cassie jumped to her feet. "Michelle! There's Comet!"

Michelle's head snapped up. She looked down the block and blinked. Her father and Stephanie were walking down the sidewalk—with Comet straining on a leash!

"Comet!" Michelle ran down the walk.

Stephanie let Comet go. He charged up the sidewalk so fast, he knocked her off her feet and into the grass.

Michelle giggled and hugged him as he licked her face. "Oh, Comet! I'm so glad to see you. Where have you been?"

"Visiting at Morrin's house," Stephanie said.

"Who's Morrin?" Michelle asked, standing up.

"It seems Comet made a dog friend at the park." Danny reached down and scratched the dog behind the ears.

"Well, that's good, because he'll be spending a lot more time playing in the park," Michelle said. "Starting today!"

"Today?" Danny frowned, puzzled. "What about the dog show? It doesn't start until one o'clock. If we leave now, we can still get there on time."

"Unh-unh." Michelle shook her head. "If I hadn't made Comet work so hard, he wouldn't have run away. I don't want him to go in the dog show if *he* doesn't want to."

Danny squatted down to look Michelle in the eye. "Comet didn't run away because of the training."

"How do you know?" Michelle asked.

"I know because Comet's a boy dog," Danny said. "And Morrin's a girl dog."

Michelle's mouth fell open. "You mean Comet's in love?"

"Yep." Danny grinned. "And after all the training you and Comet did, I think it would be a real shame not to give him the chance to go to the dog show."

"Oh. I didn't think about it like that." Michelle looked at the dog. "How about it, Comet? This may be your only chance to win a real blue ribbon."

Comet just looked at her with adoring eyes, wagging his tail and panting.

"Do you think that means yes?" Michelle looked at Stephanie and then at her dad.

"Looks like a yes to me," Stephanie said.

"Me, too." Danny stood up and cocked his head. "What do you think?"

Michelle didn't hesitate. "I think we'd better get driving. Dog show, here we come!"

Chapter
16

Stephanie stared out the front window on the drive to the Canine Center in Burnsville. She was so busy wondering what to do about Allie and Chris that she was only half listening to the conversation between Michelle and Cassie and Mandy. All three of them sat in the backseat with Comet.

"I've got butterflies in my stomach again," Michelle said.

"So do I," Mandy said. "And I don't have to go out in front of all those people."

"I'm glad my mom said I could come watch, though," Cassie put in.

"Me, too!" Mandy said.

"Me three!" Michelle added.

Comet barked in agreement.

Stephanie smiled.

"Joey said everyone gets nervous before doing something in front of an audience," Michelle said. "Do you, Dad?"

"Do I get nervous?" Danny nodded. "Yep. At seven o'clock every morning Monday through Friday."

"Yeah, well—" Michelle took a deep breath. "At least, you don't have to worry about whether or not Aunt Becky will 'sit' or 'stay' when you tell her to."

Danny laughed. "That's true. Just remember that you're going to the dog show to have fun. Win or lose, we're all proud of you, Michelle. You've done a great job with Comet the past two weeks."

"You sure have, Michelle." Stephanie turned around to smile at her sister. "I don't think I'd have the patience to keep trying with Comet the way you did."

Stephanie turned back to the window when the girls started whispering and giggling together.

What was she going to say to Allie? She had to clue her friend in on what Chris was really like before he broke her heart.

The parking lot at the Canine Center was full. Danny parked on a grassy field with a lot of other cars. Then they had to hurry to reach the registration table before it closed. Stephanie carried Michelle's backpack, which contained a dog brush, a dish for water, and two bags of treats.

Although the Canine Center had a large building for training classes, the dog show was being held outside in a white-fenced arena. Stephanie was really impressed with the setup.

Bleachers like those on the John Muir Middle School football field ran the length of the fence on the far side of the arena. A grassy area in front of the woods had been set aside for the contestants. Kids aged six to sixteen groomed and practiced with dogs ranging from ordinary mutts to registered breeds of all kinds, from tiny chihuahuas to huge Irish wolfhounds. Joey, Darcy, and Allie caught up with them just as they reached the registration table set against the building. Joey had driven Stephanie's friends in his car. Uncle Jesse and Aunt Becky had stayed home with the twins.

"This is some crowd." Joey whistled as he looked around.

The bleachers weren't full, but there were a lot more spectators than Stephanie had expected. The registration table was mobbed with late arrivals.

"Maybe Allie and Darcy and I should wait over there out of the way, Dad," Stephanie said. She pointed past the back of the line of kids waiting to register.

"Good idea," Danny agreed.

"I wonder where Chris is." Allie stood on tiptoe to see over the heads of all the people milling about as she followed Stephanie and Darcy to an empty bench set against the Canine Center building.

"Well, if Chris is in the show, he has to go there to enter the arena." Darcy pointed toward a large gate in the white fence. A few kids wearing white-and-black number cards pinned to their backs walked dogs up and down outside the arena fence.

"This is really impressive." Allie's smile stood

out in the crowd that milled around them. "I can't wait to see Chris and Jasper compete."

Stephanie couldn't stand it anymore. She hated watching Allie be fooled by that two-timing cheater! The longer she put off telling Allie about Chris, the harder it was going to be for her best friend to take.

"Listen, Allie. Can I talk to you a minute?" she asked.

"Sure. What is it?" Allie continued to scan the crowd for Chris.

"Um—I mean, can I talk to you alone?" Stephanie said.

"Wait, there's Chris!" Allie started to wave, then paused. "He doesn't see me."

"Where is he?" Darcy peered through the crowd.

Stephanie pointed as Chris and Jasper edged toward them. She could tell he didn't see them through the crowd.

Just as Allie opened her mouth to call his name, Stephanie noticed a pretty girl with long, blond hair approach Chris from behind.

"Wait, Allie," Stephanie said, putting a hand on her friend's arm.

"Why?" Allie's confused frown deepened the instant she noticed the blond girl.

The girl shifted a small poodle into the crook of one arm and tapped Chris on the shoulder.

Chris hadn't noticed Stephanie and her friends before he turned toward the blond girl, but they were close enough to hear the conversation.

"Hey, C.J. It's so good to see you again." The girl kissed him on the cheek.

Allie drew in her breath so sharply, Stephanie heard it above the hum of the crowd.

"Hi, Beverly," Chris—C.J.—said with a big smile. "How are you?"

"Just fine. I had a great time at miniature golf on Wednesday. Let's do it again sometime, okay?"

"Definitely. I'll call you next week." Chris waved as Beverly moved on.

Allie is the sweetest person in the whole world, Stephanie thought angrily. *She doesn't deserve to be treated like this.* She glanced at Allie, expecting her friend to be hurt and upset. But Allie's face was red and her eyes flashed with anger. She stormed up to Chris.

Stephanie grabbed Darcy and hurried after Allie.

Allie tapped Chris on the shoulder just the way Beverly had. He turned with a grin—and froze when he saw Allie.

"Allie," Chris squeaked. "What are you doing here?"

Stephanie and Darcy stood behind her. Stephanie didn't know what Allie intended to do, but she wanted to be there to support her friend.

"You *invited* me, remember, Chris?" Allie was sweet, but she wasn't a doormat. Right now she was hurt and angry.

"I did?" Chris shrugged. "Guess I forgot. But since you're here, we could—"

"Are you serious? You told me you were training Jasper on Wednesday. Not playing miniature golf with another girl! You are such a jerk!"

"Allie, I can explain," Chris said.

"Don't bother!" Allie's eyes flashed. "I wouldn't go out with you again if you were the only boy in San Francisco. Good-bye."

Yes! Stephanie smiled with satisfaction. Chris had trapped himself and Allie had told him off

137

before he made a total fool of her! *Even better*, she thought with relief. *I'm not the one who had to tell her that Chris was going out with other girls.*

"Stephanie!" Michelle's voice carried through the crowd. "Look what I got!"

Stephanie saw the white card with the black number twenty-three that Michelle waved with pride. She gave her a hearty thumbs-up. Now that Allie was free of her two-timing boyfriend, they could all enjoy the dog show.

As long as Michelle and Comet don't totally mess up! Stephanie thought, crossing her fingers.

Chapter
17

Michelle stood near the gate with the other kids in the beginner obedience class. There were twenty contestants waiting with their dogs—even though it wouldn't be their turn until after the advanced class. Michelle was really nervous and tightened her grip on Comet's leash. Comet looked up at her with worried eyes.

Michelle patted his head. "It's okay, boy. We're gonna be fine. Honest."

After his night out with Morrin, Comet looked a little scruffier than most of the other dogs, even though she had brushed him. There hadn't been time to give him another bath.

"I don't believe it, Michelle. You actually showed up."

Michelle recognized Rachel's voice and turned slowly. *Don't let her get to you,* she coached herself. *Just stay cool and calm.*

"Hi, Rachel. You're not in our class, are you?" Michelle asked.

"No!" Rachel scoffed. She looked down at Bonnie Blue. "Bonnie is in the advanced class."

And, boy, am I glad to hear that! Michelle thought. She and Comet didn't have any chance of winning a ribbon against Rachel's dog. *Bonnie Blue does everything right all the time.*

"So I guess you're not going in the just-for-fun classes, then, either, are you?" Michelle asked out loud.

"I wouldn't at a regular dog show, but this Children's Dog Show is different." Rachel looked around. "I could use a few more blue ribbons on the bulletin board in my bedroom. It should be easy for Bonnie to win the fun classes."

That didn't seem fair to Michelle, but she didn't say anything. The program her father had gotten at the registration table said that the fun classes had been included to give everyone a chance to compete and win—even family pets that didn't have any real training.

"Well, I brought Comet here to have fun," Michelle said. "We don't really care about winning."

"That's good," Rachel said. "Because you won't."

Michelle just shrugged. She had learned a long time ago that Rachel wouldn't bother her as long as she didn't get mad or upset. Keeping her feelings inside wasn't easy, but it worked.

"I have to get closer to the gate." Rachel started off with Bonnie at her side. "See you later, Michelle."

"Sure. Whatever." Michelle patted the Baggie full of treats she had in her pocket. She didn't care if she lost points for using them. Comet would try harder and behave better if she gave him a reward. She still wanted to win a ribbon, but now that she was here, she didn't think she had much of a chance. Mostly, she just hoped she and Comet didn't totally mess up.

The announcer and three judges sat at a table in a covered stand at the far end of the arena.

The sides of the stand looked just like the fence, and it was raised above the fence on legs so they all had a good view of the contestants in the arena.

When the announcer called the first contestant into the arena, Michelle moved up to the fence to watch. The advanced dogs were really impressive. When the contest was over, the announcer called out the winners. Allie's friend—Christopher James Nelson—and Jasper won the blue ribbon. Rachel and Bonnie Blue got a second-place red. Rachel did not look happy.

When all the advanced contestants had left the arena, Michelle took a deep breath and looked around at the other beginners. *There are other kids here who look just as scared as I am*, she thought. She glanced toward the stands. Joey, Stephanie, Allie, and Darcy were sitting one row up behind her father, Cassie, and Mandy. They all waved. Danny gave her a thumbs-up.

The announcer called the first beginner into the arena.

Michelle moved closer to the gate. The beginner pattern for the basic commands was easier than the advanced pattern. And the man giving directions stayed in the ring to help anyone who couldn't remember what to do.

Then the announcer called, "Number twenty-three, Michelle Tanner and Comet!"

Michelle took a deep breath and shortened Comet's leash. Then she gave him a treat from her pocket. "This is it, boy. Come on."

Michelle thought it would be easy to run Comet over to the starting line for the pattern. *Wrong!* She had worried about herself being nervous in front of a lot of people. It had never occurred to her that Comet might be scared. He stopped ten feet into the arena and wouldn't budge.

"Comet!" Michelle whispered, pulling on the leash. "Come on, boy. It's okay."

A few people in the stands started laughing.

"This is a *Children's* dog show," the announcer said. "Take your time, Miss Tanner."

Michelle felt her cheeks warm, but she wasn't going to give up. She looked at her dog. Poor Comet was just scared. She took a treat out of her pocket and placed her hands on both sides of his head so he was looking directly in her eyes.

"I'm right here, Comet. And I'm so happy

that you're back and safe and that you didn't run away because you were mad at me. So who cares about a stupid ribbon as long as we have each other?"

Comet licked Michelle's face, and she grinned.

"Now, come on! Let's just have fun!" Michelle showed him the treat and backed up the way she did when they played tag. Comet jumped up and ran after her.

The crowd cheered.

Michelle relaxed.

Even Comet seemed to be over his stage fright. He sat at an angle by her side and to the front instead of straight by her side the way he was supposed to. His eyes were fastened on her treat pocket.

At least he's sitting! Michelle put another treat in her hand to keep his attention on her and not on the scary crowd.

"Are you ready?" the man giving directions asked.

Michelle nodded.

"Then begin."

"Heel, Comet!" Michelle patted her leg with her hand and started walking straight ahead.

Comet pranced at her side. He stayed with her when she made a right turn at the mark, but after a few more paces, he jumped in front of her and barked. She gave him the treat, stepped around him, and kept walking.

"Heel, Comet."

Comet stayed with her until the next turn. Then he dashed in front of her again, sat down, and barked.

"Comet!" Michelle gave him another treat, then pulled several more out of her pocket so she had them handy.

"Halt!" the director ordered.

Michelle stopped and pointed to the ground—the signal for Comet to sit.

Comet didn't sit down. He stood looking around the huge arena. Michelle gave the judge a wide smile and pushed down on Comet's rump. Finally Comet sat.

Some of the people in the crowd laughed again. Michelle smiled, shrugged, and patted Comet on the head.

The only way Michelle could keep Comet going through the rest of the pattern was to feed him a treat every few feet. They actually made it around the white cones in a figure eight, and when she halted the second time, he sat without being told.

The crowd roared as Michelle and Comet jogged out of the arena. Her father was waiting at the gate.

"Michelle, that was great!" Danny gave her a huge hug.

"Well, not really," Michelle said cheerfully. "I don't think we got one thing right."

"I know, but you did the best you could, and you looked like you were having a good time."

Michelle grinned. "I was! Once I got over being nervous." *But that's not going to win us a ribbon,* she thought with a twinge of sadness.

By the time the biscuit-catching class came along, Rachel's Bonnie Blue had won another second-place ribbon, and the boy called Chris got fourth place with his black poodle, Jasper.

Michelle hadn't put Comet in the most handsome dog class because he looked so scruffy. But now it was time for the biscuit class, her one real hope of getting a ribbon.

Even a green sixth place would be nice.

Michelle led Comet into the arena with thirty

other dogs and high hopes. The judges had come down into the arena for this class. The dogs were called up three at a time to stand by one of the three judges. Each owner was given ten broken bits of biscuit, and the judges counted the ones each dog caught.

Michelle and Comet were in the second group of six. She put the ten pieces in her hand and breathed in deeply.

Comet sat perfectly still in front of her.

"Okay, boy. This is your big chance. I *know* you can do this."

The judge standing beside her smiled. "Start whenever you're ready, Miss Tanner."

Michelle held the biscuit so Comet could see it. "Okay, Comet. Catch!" She tossed it right to him.

Comet caught it!

And then he spit it out.

Michelle tried again.

Comet caught the second biscuit, then dropped it.

Michelle looked at the judge. "I don't think he likes these treats, Mr. Judge."

The man had his hand over his mouth. He

was trying hard not to laugh. "I'm sorry, but everyone has to use the same biscuits."

"Oh." Michelle sighed. She couldn't argue if that was the rule. She didn't want to be a poor sport.

The third biscuit bounced off Comet's nose because he didn't even try. By the time Michelle tossed the tenth and final piece, he was lying down, taking another nap. The crowd laughed and cheered.

Comet had scored two in the biscuit catch. The only class she and Comet had left was beginner agility.

Michelle left the arena with Comet prancing happily behind her. She couldn't help but smile at him. "It's a good thing you don't know how to be embarrassed!" she told him.

Rachel and Bonnie Blue walked out behind her. "Bonnie caught all ten biscuits. How many did Comet catch?"

"Not very many. Comet didn't like those biscuits," Michelle explained.

"That's too bad," Rachel said. "This class was probably your only hope of winning a ribbon, huh? I mean, a green ribbon isn't great, but at least you would have had *something* to take home."

"The show isn't over yet," Michelle said.

"Right." Rachel walked away, shaking her head.

Michelle watched her go. She'd been having such a good time with Comet that she'd forgotten how much of a pain Rachel could be.

There's no chance Comet will do well in agility, Michelle thought glumly. *I guess Rachel is going to make fun of me in school for the next month. So much for Comet's big day!*

Chapter
18

That is just so infuriating!" Allie huffed. "I mean, I can't even believe it!" She sat between Darcy and Stephanie up in the spectator stands.

Danny and Joey had taken Cassie and Mandy to the refreshment stand for a hot dog and a drink. Stephanie felt sorry for her best friend, but her mind was on Michelle.

Her little sister was sitting under a tree at the edge of the woods, brushing Comet. *It's too bad the dog show doesn't have a good-sportsmanship award, because Michelle would win that hands down*, Stephanie thought.

"What's infuriating?" Darcy asked Allie.

"That Chris might win the high point ribbon for the best dog overall in the advanced division." Allie shook her head. "He's such a jerk, he doesn't deserve it. And he's so snotty about it."

Stephanie had to agree with Allie. Chris was so confident that Jasper was going to win that it was maddening.

"Well, guess who has a good chance to beat him." Darcy sat back and folded her arms. "Rachel."

"I don't believe I'm going to say this, but I think Chris may be more annoying than Rachel," Allie commented.

"Chris is worse than annoying," Stephanie said. "He's a jerk."

"That's the truth." Darcy shook her head. "What a rat!"

"Well, at least, I found out before I got myself into a really embarrassing situation." Allie leaned forward with her arms resting on her knees. "Thank goodness nobody at school knew he was running around on me."

"Well, that's not quite true." Stephanie swallowed hard. Even though Allie had found out about Chris on her own, Stephanie felt guilty for not having the nerve to tell her the truth sooner.

"Someone knew?" Allie looked horrified. "Who?"

"I did," Stephanie said. "Since last week."

Allie frowned. "I don't understand. How could you possibly know? I mean, you never met Chris before today, right?"

Stephanie poured out the whole story of how she had met "C.J." at the park, how he had offered to help her train Comet, and how she had really wanted to go out with him. "When he asked me to go out with him Saturday, I didn't know he was your boyfriend, Allie."

"When did you find out?" Darcy asked.

"When I took Alex to the rest room at the mall last Friday." Stephanie felt lower than low. "I saw Allie and Chris go into the Game Arcade together."

"When did you go out with him, then?" Allie asked.

Stephanie was relieved to hear that Allie didn't sound mad, just confused.

"I never went out with him," Stephanie explained. "I was supposed to go to the movies with C.J. on Saturday, but after I saw you together on Friday, I canceled."

"Saturday?" Allie's face clouded with fury. "Chris told me he had a family thing he couldn't get out of on Saturday. But he really had a date with you!"

Stephanie winced. "I don't blame you for being mad at me, Allie, but—"

"Mad at *you?*" Allie cried. "Why would I be mad at you? I mean, I don't blame you for wanting to go out with him, Stephanie. He's totally charming."

"Until you get to know the rat within," Darcy added.

"A major, lying rat." Allie looked totally furious.

"I'm really sorry, Allie," Stephanie said. "But I'm glad I told you the truth. I hated lying to you last week when I knew what a jerk he was. I was just afraid you wouldn't believe me, or you'd be mad that I was saying bad things about your boyfriend."

Allie smiled. "No way, Steph. Boyfriends come and go, but best friends are always there for you. I'd never be mad at you for telling me the truth."

"Well, I'll always tell you the truth from now on," Stephanie promised.

Relieved, she looked back toward the grassy staging area. Michelle wasn't brushing Comet now. She was just sitting and petting him.

"I think Michelle could use a pep talk." Stephanie stood up. "You guys don't mind if I leave for a while, do you?"

"Of course not," Darcy said. "And tell Michelle she shouldn't feel bad. As far as I'm concerned, she and Comet have been the best thing in this dog show."

"I think so, too," Allie said. "She should feel proud. For a family pet, Comet has done great."

"I'll tell her. Thanks." Feeling better now that she had confessed to Allie, Stephanie made her way down to the floor. She bought a can of cold soda from a vendor and went directly to the staging area.

Michelle was staring into space. She didn't look up until Stephanie spoke. "I brought you a soda. I thought you might be thirsty after all that work today."

"Thanks, Stephanie." Michelle popped the top and took a long drink. "But I feel like I totally let you and Dad and everyone else in the family down."

"That is absolutely not true." Stephanie sat on the grass beside her. "I'm really proud of you, Michelle. I bet you're the only kid here who trained her dog without any professional help. That counts for a lot."

"Yeah, but—" Michelle sighed. "I really wanted a ribbon. Comet probably won't even *finish* the agility course."

"Maybe not, but you and Comet have won something better than a ribbon," Stephanie said.

"What?"

"Everyone in the audience loves you! Allie and Darcy both said you and Comet were the best thing in the whole show."

"Really?" Michelle looked doubtful. "But everybody is laughing at us. Even the judge!"

"There's nothing awful about making people laugh," Stephanie said. "People love to laugh, and people love you and Comet."

Michelle started to smile. "Are you just trying to make me feel better?"

"Yeah. Is it working?" Stephanie asked.

Michelle grinned broadly and gave her a thumbs-up.

"Cool!" Stephanie replied.

"Contestants for the beginner agility class, on deck, please," the announcer said.

"That's us, Comet!" Michelle leaned over to shake the dog awake. "Wake up!"

Comet yawned, stretched, and slowly got to his feet.

Stephanie gave Michelle a high-five and stood up.

"Agility course, here we come," Michelle said.

With a smile Stephanie watched her go. Sometimes being the older sister wasn't so bad. Especially when the younger sister was a *real* winner.

Chapter 19

Danny, Joey, Mandy, and Cassie were waiting for Michelle by the gate.

"There you are!" Danny gave her a big hug. "That's for luck."

"Believe me, I'll need it." Michelle took a deep breath.

Comet sat down beside her in the heel position. Joey reached out and patted his head. "What a dog!"

"Rachel won again," Mandy said. "In the advanced agility class."

"Well, Bonnie Blue is a great dog," Michelle said.

"Right." Cassie sighed. "And that's all Rachel's going to talk about for the next month."

Good, Michelle thought. *Then maybe she won't talk about me.*

The announcer called the first contestant into the arena for the beginner agility class. "Number fourteen. Jason Payne and his dog, Wild Bill."

"I guess this is it, Michelle." Danny hung back when Joey, Cassie, and Mandy left to go back to their seats. "I just want you to know that I am so proud of you, I could bust."

Michelle giggled. "Thanks, Dad. And guess what?"

"What?"

"I'm having fun!"

"Then I'm even prouder," Danny said.

Michelle waved as her dad went back to the bleachers. She listened closely as the director explained the course to Jason Payne and tried to memorize it. *Jumps, ramp, weaving things, and tunnel.* She took another deep breath and tried to relax while she waited for her turn.

Michelle had talked to a couple of the kids in the grassy staging area and found out that it had taken months to teach their dogs agility.

"It was totally unfair of me to think you could learn it in two weeks, Comet." Michelle scratched her dog behind the ears. "I'm sorry."

Comet cocked his head and looked at her lovingly.

Then the announcer called her number. "Michelle Tanner and Comet!"

"Come on, boy!" Michelle checked her pocket to make sure she had plenty of treats. "Let's go have some real fun!"

When Michelle and Comet entered the arena, the crowd began to applaud. Michelle knew there was no way Comet was going to run the agility course for real. "We might as well give everyone a good show, right?"

Comet sat, waiting.

Michelle unclipped his leash and dropped it, then grabbed a fistful of treats. "Ready?"

Comet barked and danced around her.

"Set! Go!" Michelle took off toward the jumps with Comet loping close behind. She sailed over the first low rail and stopped when she heard the crowd start to laugh. She looked back to see Comet crawling under the rail just like he did at home. "Perfect."

When he was clear, Michelle got down and crawled under the second jump.

Comet leaped over it.

A cheer rose up from the crowd.

She gave him a treat and ran on to the ramp. The obstacle was a ramp on only one side. It had steps on the other. Since Comet was used to going up and down stairs at home, she went up the steps first, and then down the ramp.

Comet went up the steps, stopped to stare at the ramp, then went back down the steps.

Michelle threw up her hands and tossed him a treat.

Everyone in the bleachers laughed.

Palming another Beefy-Bite, Michelle ran to the white cones and wove in and out around them the way her dog was supposed to.

Comet just barreled on by the cones and sat down in front of Michelle to wait for his treat.

"Now, there's a dog with a mind of his own," the announcer said. "I guess we know who's the boss in the Tanner house."

The crowd whistled and clapped louder.

Michelle dropped down on all fours and started to crawl through the tunnel. The only time Comet had made it through the canvas tunnel at home was when Mandy and Cassie had pushed him through. Michelle kept waiting for the dog to appear at the other end just like he did in the backyard. She couldn't believe it when she crawled out and Comet crawled out behind her.

Michelle jumped to her feet. "He did it! He did it!" She gave Comet a quick hug, his treat, and then ran toward the gate.

The crowd was on its feet, applauding.

"And that's our last contestant for the day," the announcer said. "Let's have the whole beginner agility class back into the arena for the awards. Everyone else, please, have your dogs on deck for the high point awards. And I mean everyone."

Michelle picked up Comet's leash and clipped it to his collar. She looked toward the stands as she walked into the center of the arena with the other kids and dogs. Her father, Joey, Stephanie, and their friends were all standing up with their fists raised in victory.

"Well, Comet, we didn't win a ribbon, but we were a big hit. I guess that's pretty good for two weeks' work."

Michelle got in line and waited patiently until the six ribbons were awarded. When she started to leave, the director told everyone to stay for the high point awards. All the kids and dogs that had been in the show came into the arena to wait.

The crowd and all the contestants grew quiet when one of the judges gave a piece of paper to the announcer.

Rachel sidled up next to Michelle. "You know you can't do stuff like that in a real dog show."

"That's okay," Michelle said. "Comet and I are going to retire." *This was fun*, she thought, *and I'm glad I did it, but I think Comet would rather be a happy family dog than a show dog.*

Comet shoved his nose in her treat pocket. Michelle gave him two Beefy-Bits.

A grade-school boy with a small terrier won the high point ribbon for the fun events. A high school girl with an ordinary mutt took high point for beginners.

Michelle turned to look at Rachel and noticed Chris standing just beyond her with a smug grin on his face. The grin turned to a look of shocked disbelief when the announcer called out Rachel as the high point winner in the advanced category.

"Yay, Rachel!" Michelle applauded along with everyone else. Even she thought Bonnie Blue was the best-trained dog in the show.

"Thanks, Michelle. This is so great!" Rachel ran forward to get her ribbon.

Chris stormed off toward the gate with Jasper and didn't come back, even when the announcer said there was one more award.

No wonder Stephanie didn't seem to like him, Michelle thought. Chris was a poor loser!

"The judges will present the last award of the first annual Children's Dog Show," the announcer said.

One of the judges came down from the announcer's stand with a gleaming silver trophy in his hand. The top was shaped like a stemmed goblet with two handles. It stood about twelve inches high on a marble base.

"What are they giving a trophy for?" Rachel asked when she got back with her high point ribbon.

"I don't know." Michelle was curious, too.

"The winner of the trophy for 'The dog the

judges would most like to take home' is . . . Comet Tanner!"

The crowd cheered.

Rachel gasped. "What?"

Michelle blinked. *Did he say Comet Tanner?*

"Come on, Michelle!" The announcer laughed. "Our judges don't make mistakes."

A trophy? Dazed, Michelle tugged on Comet and walked toward the smiling judge. *I wanted a ribbon and Comet won a trophy!*

All the judges congratulated Michelle and thanked her for making the Children's Dog Show the fun event they had intended it to be.

Still dazed, Michelle mumbled her thanks and turned toward the gate. Her friends and family were waiting when she came out clutching the silver trophy to her chest.

"Will you look at that?" Joey started to take the trophy and paused. "Can I hold it?"

Michelle nodded and let him take it.

"We'll have to find a special place to put this baby." Joey held the trophy up and nodded. "In the living room. Definitely in the living room."

"That's my girl!" Her father kissed her on the cheek and hugged her. "You won a trophy!"

"Well, not really, Dad. Comet won the trophy!" Michelle squatted down and threw her arms around the bewildered dog.

"Yes, he did," Danny said. "But I don't think Comet will appreciate having a trophy as much as you will. I noticed that the supply store here has a doghouse just like the one we saw at Anderson's Dog Training School last week."

"They do?" Michelle stared at her dad.

Danny nodded, then grinned. "So let's buy it for Comet as a reward for a job well done!"

"Whoa! Thanks, Dad!" Michelle squatted down and hugged Comet. "Did you hear that, boy? Dad's going to get you the best doghouse in the whole world!"

Comet licked Michelle's face.

"This is so cool." Stephanie squatted down beside Michelle and laughed when Comet licked her, too. "I have to confess, Michelle. I didn't think you could do it."

"That's okay, Stephanie." Michelle grinned. "This is your trophy just as much as it is mine and Comet's."

"How do you figure that?" Stephanie asked.

"Easy," Michelle said. "If *you* hadn't tried to

train Comet and gotten him all confused, *I* might have made more progress. Then Comet would have been just another boring dog instead of the star of the show!"

Stephanie hesitated, then nodded. "Well, I guess it takes *two* sisters to make a winning dog after all!"

Don't miss out on any of
Stephanie and Michelle's
exciting adventures!

FULL HOUSE™
Sisters

When sisters get together...
expect the unexpected!

 A MINSTREL® BOOK

Published by Pocket Books

2012-05

It doesn't matter if you live around the corner...
or around the world...
If you are a fan of Mary-Kate and Ashley Olsen,
you should be a member of

MARY-KATE + ASHLEY'S FUN CLUB™

Here's what you get:
Our Funzine™
An autographed color photo
Two black & white individual photos
A full size color poster
An official **Fun Club**™ membership card
A **Fun Club**™ school folder
Two special **Fun Club**™ surprises
A holiday card
Fun Club™ collectibles catalog
Plus a **Fun Club**™ box to keep everything in

To join Mary-Kate + Ashley's Fun Club™, fill out the form
below and send it along with

U.S. Residents – $17.00
Canadian Residents – $22 U.S. Funds
International Residents – $27 U.S. Funds

MARY-KATE + ASHLEY'S FUN CLUB™
859 HOLLYWOOD WAY, SUITE 275
BURBANK, CA 91505

NAME:_____

ADDRESS:_____

_CITY:_____ STATE:_____ ZIP:_____

PHONE:(____) _____ BIRTHDATE:_____

TM & © 1996 Dualstar Entertainment Group, Inc.   1242